VIRTUAL LIES

JD COMBS

Perfect Mamas Press
Richmond, Virginia Edition

COPYRIGHT 2013, 2016 JD COMBS

This work is licensed under a Creative Commons Attribution-Noncommercial-No Derivative Works 3.0 Unported License.

Attribution — You must attribute the work in the manner specified by the author or licensor (but not in any way that suggests that they endorse you or your use of the work).

Noncommercial — You may not use this work for commercial purposes.

No Derivative Works — You may not alter, transform, or build upon this work.

Inquiries about additional permissions
should be directed to: jcp8675309@live.com

Cover Design by Rebecca Poole
Edited by Vicki Sly
Proofread by Amy Oravec

Previously self-published 2013 as *The Point of No Return*

This is a work of fiction. Names, characters, places, brands, media, and incidents are either the product of the author's imagination or are used fictitiously. Any resemblance to similarly named places or to persons living or deceased is unintentional.

CONTENTS

Prologue 7

Chapter One 9

Chapter Two 37

Chapter Three 51

Chapter Four 66

Chapter Five 84

Chapter Six 95

Chapter Seven 105

Chapter Eight 125

Chapter Nine 144

Chapter Ten 151

Chapter Eleven 177

Epilogue 183

*To those who love me, support me
and hold me to a higher standard,
I couldn't have done this without you.*

*It's been a wild ride, and I can't wait to do it again
with each of you by my side. xo*

PROLOGUE

HE SITS STARING at the computer screen, mesmerized by the images. The folder of pictures contains hundreds, maybe thousands, of pictures of beautiful women—all sent to him, no one else, just him. He can't help but feel the rush of power and excitement that comes from knowing these photos are his alone, taken for him or by him.

His wife wouldn't have dreamed of sending him pictures like this, even before her accident. She is too straight-laced and uptight to think about sending a provocative, sex-filled picture of herself. Sometimes, though, he likes to lean back and pretend it is his wife on the computer screen in front of him. How different life would be if his wife could send these types of images. Sometimes, he almost mourns the life he has lost, but then his mind replays the phone calls, the Skype chats, the pictures, and the excitement he feels at the thought of heading out of town for his business meetings. Any sadness quickly fades into the background with the knowledge that his wife would never be the women in these pictures.

He has a new one now—a new addition to his collection. He calls them his collectibles. They are his beautiful, collectible dolls that become his playthings. He can justify them that way. There is no talk of love or a future—just play. Sometimes, the playfulness can lead to physical pleasure but never love. He has some training to do with the new girl. In theory, she gets the concept of playing with him, but reality is a different matter. The e-mail from her proves this point. She seems a little too naïve, in a way, to adhere to his rules. She's trying to set her own rules. Just for a laugh, he rereads her e-mail …

"You set down your ground rules. I gave you a sketchy outline of what I expected, but you overwhelmed me a little with your rules. Sooooo, here are my ground rules. I'm (usually) a very honest person. This is all new to me. But I'll be up front with you when things get overwhelming for me, which I'm sure they will.

Yes, flirt. Be fun with me. Have fun with me. I'll do the same with you.

Being physical with you is something I can't consider. Kisses lead to intimacy with me. Intimacy leads to feelings. Feelings lead to problems. I'm not interested in giving, or receiving, sloppy seconds.

So, text away, but they're my rules now, Skippy. If you want to come along for a flirty, fun little time, jump on board. If my rules are too much, then you are free to go back to the way things were before. Friends always."

Oh, she so doesn't understand this is my game, and these are my rules. She will need to learn, and it will be so much fun teaching her. First things first, time to make the deal even more attractive. Time to get her number and make her part of his collection. He needs to add her pictures to his gallery.

He logs into Facebook and brings up the messages from the previous night. Hers are at the top of the list. Seeing she is online, he takes the opportunity to pounce on his latest prey.

Him:
Hey there. This is going to scare you, but I need you to call me. I have something I really need to talk to you about. My number is 523-732-7462.

He waits for the immediate response she usually gives him. It seems like it is taking her an eternity to respond when he notices she has gone.

Him:
Oh, you're gone …

With that, he shifts gears. He is no longer a man on the prowl. He is in professional mode. It's time to make the money flow for himself and others. It's time to work.

CHAPTER ONE

MARCH 8

How did things get so bad? OK, maybe bad is the wrong word. Maybe it's just not what I expected. I have a good life, from the outside, anyway. Anyone looking in would think I have the picture-perfect world. My life makes me think of the song He Thinks He'll Keep Her by Mary Chapin Carpenter. In the song she, talks about how the wife works to keep things looking picture-perfect "spit and polish till it shines," but she falls out of love, maybe because of the monotony of her daily life. Or maybe it's because she didn't get much recognition for who she is as a woman and a lover, only as a mom and a wife. I think I'm becoming the girl in the song.

I know things aren't really that bad. Garrett doesn't abuse me or cheat on me (at least not that I know of). But we rarely talk anymore. The laughter is gone. It's been replaced with apathy. Where there was once passion, laughter, and a shared ideal about building a life together, now there is only indifference. The TV is the moderator in our marriage. As long as the TV is on, there are no conflicts. I have to wonder how, with no work being put into our marriage, he thinks he'll keep me.

I have to admit I'm partly to blame for all of this. I used to be the one to pick fights, to try and draw out what was wrong between us and fix the problems. But I got so tired of feeling like a nag, so I stopped. It was always up to me change the dynamic between us. Garrett has always been happy to bury his head in the sand and let problems go. In our early years, I brought up our issues to Garrett. He used to sit and talk with me. He wanted to look interested in fixing our marital bumps, but life always went back to the way Garrett wanted it. If he wanted to change things, he would fix them, but if they were my issues, everything always went back to the way it was before. It was exhausting and unrewarding work, so I stopped. I always hoped, though, Garrett would see how our marriage is becoming empty, and he would want to help mend our blended hearts before it was too late.

I know life could be so much worse, and I feel like a shrew as I sit here thinking, "Oh, woe is me!" So, I'll take a break from my pity party and try to focus on the positive. The kids are my positive and my world.

As long as I focus on their five beautiful faces, life is more than bearable. My darlings take my breath away when I look at them. I am in awe of what a gorgeous, young woman Christina is. At 16, she's in charge of her world and not afraid to show it. It's scary to think how confident she is. She'll do big things in her life. Noelle, sweet little Noelle, with her halo of blonde hair, she's quiet and bookish unless she's with Andrew. Andrew pulls her out of her shell. His boisterousness is combined with an unrivaled sensitivity. I love seeing them together. And the twins, Amanda and Chandler, crack me up with their bickering banter back and forth. Those two are like a little old couple. I am in heaven when all of my kids are around.

It's really only Garrett. He's the void, the empty space in my life. If I let my mind wander back in time, my heart hurts. I see a man and a husband who used to think the world of me, but that feeling is disappearing day by day. The joy we shared together is gone. Life is flat.

Our marriage is mediocre, at best, and teetering on divorce, at worst. Sometimes, I wonder why, if it used to be so good, we let it get to the point of being nearly irreparable. But then I remember the hurt, the pain from so many years of unresolved conflicts. I see the lack of trying, on Garrett's part, to make things better. I feel I always come last with him.

Charley closes her journal, logs into her computer, and tries to drift back to happy times gone by. There is not much there, inside Charley's heart, when she looks at pictures of their early days. Their wedding album used to fill her with delight, but now looking at it only serves to remind her she will never be able to compete with her mother-in-law. *Will he keep me? Or is it too late?* Charley's mind starts to churn as words come spilling forth, and she picks up her journal again and begins to write ...

The Questions

The questions I have, there are so many.
The answers—I'm afraid, right now, there aren't any.
They'll come from within, only answered by me.

Right now, there is nothing for me to give, you see.
My heart is so heavy, so hurt.
Not a thing can be done for the pain to avert.
Did I love you with all of my heart?
Or did I just love the thought of "us" from the start?
We seemed so perfect, so right.
Everything was wonderful. You were my knight.
Did I do the right thing?
Did I just want a ring?
Did I rush you?
What did I do?
I didn't want to be alone.
Oh, how I wish I had known.
Was this the path I was supposed to choose?
Or did I choose the path where we both lose?
I don't know which end is up or down.
I feel I am ready to drown.
This is not the right life for you or for me.
This is not right, not for either to be.
We are full of despair and not at all right.
I want it back to when we filled each other with delight.

We ...

Charley lays down her pen. *Will the "we" continue?* She puts away her journal, tucks the memories of the pictures into the back of her head, and vows to shake off her mental whining.

* * *

March 9
I thought today dawned a little brighter. At least it seemed that way at first. Garrett wasn't so distant and reserved. He seemed more "in the moment" as he walked into the kitchen with a cheery "Good morning" and a kiss on my lips. He snuck a quick hug and a little fondle into the routine of the morning, so I thought maybe I'm just imagining big problems where there really aren't any.

But life went back to normal when Garrett got himself ready to leave for work. He sat at the kitchen table, staring at his iPhone. He got lost in the texts and e-mails as they came in. As is the case every morning, I worked around Garrett, getting the kids fed, lunches made, and everyone out the door. Garrett was the last to leave, and he placed a perfunctory kiss on my forehead. I was left standing in the door, a bit bewildered, wondering what happened to the sweetness that greeted me this morning. He, half-heartedly, waved good-bye and headed down the street, off to work. Maybe it's just the pressures of the job. I hope, sometimes fervently, the problems in our marriage don't stem from our life together. Maybe, hopefully, it's just his job.

Charley closes her journal and wanders back into the silence of the kitchen to get to work on cleaning up and setting things back to normal.

Once the kitchen is restored and gleaming, Charley decides it's time for her to catch up on the virtual world, and she logs into Facebook. She scrolls down the list of updates from her friends, commenting here and there on things that catch her attention. She is messaging back and forth with her best friend, Gayle Myers, when a friend request pops up on her screen. Charley clicks on it and is immediately transported back in time to high school. Peter Pampinelli. Hmm ... she wonders, why is he "friending" me? She knows it's not because they were the best of friends in high school. Their paths rarely, if ever, crossed.

Charley was among the bookish, quiet crowd. Peter was a cool, aloof, artsy type. He reminded her so much of Johnny Depp from the movie *Benny and Joon*. He was a little different, but he didn't care. He was self-assured in a way that most high school boys weren't. Charley remembers seeing him at two of their first high school reunions and thinking he had become more beautiful. He had filled out through the shoulders and chest. His wavy hair dipped across his forehead, making his tawny eyes stand out. Charley thinks back to one of their first get togethers after high school and being intrigued by the aloofness he emanated, which only added to his mystique. With excitement bubbling up, she messages Gayle about the new friend request. And then Charley pulls out her old yearbooks.

Charley reminisces flipping through the pages. She thinks back to when he moved into the town where they grew up. They were in sixth grade, and she remembers being in awe of his swarthy, dark, Italian looks. She loved the way he spoke Italian in school to the girls who ran in his crowd. His dad was an Italian professor at the University of Michigan, so the Italian was true to who he was. But she is sure he used those sweet-sounding words to his advantage. She flips to the index, and his senior picture stuns her. He has braces, but other than that, he is nearly flawless. His hair is dark and wavy, curling back from his forehead. His tawny brown eyes seem to sparkle with a mischievous glint shining through the decades-old paper. His high cheekbones and big broad smile are finished off with a strong jaw and cleft chin.

She flips further and further into her old yearbook and sees him on the pages of all of the theatrical performances. She didn't realize, though, that he was also on the golf and basketball teams. As Charley turns to old pictures of herself on the pages of clubs, not sports or theater, she has to wonder why he would friend her across the virtual world of Facebook. Charley feels like she has been transported back to high school with her reaction to his friend request. Her heartbeat is a little more rapid than usual, and she can feel heat flood her cheeks with color. She is not used to being friended by former high school classmates on Facebook, especially a request from a gorgeous man who is her old secret crush. She abandons instant messaging and grabs the phone to pick Gayle's brain.

"What should I do, Gayle? Should I play it cool and accept it, or should I play it cooler and ignore it for a while?" Charley wonders.

Gayle bursts out laughing, "You are acting just like you're a boy-crazy high school girl. You're forty-two years old, and you're acting like you have zero confidence in yourself to make a decision. It's a friend request, for heaven's sake, not an invitation to go to prom! Just friend him and be done with it, or ignore it and move on."

"But Gayle, you haven't seen him. He's beautiful, and he's asking to be my friend. God, I had such a crush on him in high school," Charley tries to explain.

Gayle cuts her off before she can go any further, "You haven't seen him, either. You're looking at a picture from twenty-four years ago. For all you know, he could have turned to mush and lost all of his hair. He could be a thousand-pound manatee with no friends."

Charley knows Gayle is right, but she still can't shake the image of Peter Pampinelli asking to be her friend. So, she does what any self-respecting woman with a friend request from a hot, old classmate would do—she hangs up with Gayle, and she checks him out on Facebook. She goes on to his page and looks through his pictures.

Damn, he hasn't changed much. He's a little gray around the temples, but his hair is still dark and wavy. His eyes are still sparkly and mischievous. The high cheekbones are still there, in a mostly unlined face, and are now made even more stunning without the braces. He hasn't gained a pound. His shoulders are broad, and his waist is narrow. He is beautiful. Wow!

Feeling a little stalker-ish, Charley shuts down Facebook and turns her attention to work, vowing to wait a day on accepting Peter's friend request.

* * *

Garrett returns home from work as distracted as when he'd left. Charley tries hard to pull him into her world, but he is engrossed in his phone, the TV and, to a minor extent, the kids. There is little recognition that Charley is even there. Garrett makes small talk with the twins as they sit at the kitchen counter finishing their homework. Charley tries hard to interject and engage, but her words are drowned out by a child, phone calls, e-mails and, as always, texts to be answered by Garrett.

Charley retreats to the world in her mind as she prepares dinner for their family—a place filled with love and laughter. In her head she could replay, over and over, the good, wonderful, and perfect times she and Garrett created in their past. In her mind she could make herself remember why she's still here. In her mind, she focuses on the kids and love—the kind of love she used to have.

With dinner done and the kids cleaning the kitchen, Garrett heads to the TV room to watch a little Thursday night football. *Again, with the TV,* Charley thinks. "I can't compete," she muses out loud. Andrew, their true middle child—the one who wears his heart on his sleeve and tries desperately to always please everyone—hears her and asks what she means.

Charley turns to face her son, working hard to wipe away any trace of sadness from her face and says, "I was just talking to myself about not being able to compete with Gayle in an upcoming race."

As hard as she tries to hide her melancholy, Andrew picks up a vibe that something is not quite right and walks over to envelope Charley in the biggest bear hug his twelve-year-old arms can give. Charley laughs as Andrew threatens to throw her off balance, but she revels in the closeness and love she feels with her son's embrace, counting her blessings by looking at each and every one of her children.

As Charley shoos Andrew back to his chores, she goes to join Garrett in the TV room, hoping maybe her presence will break him away from a football game that just a few years ago wouldn't have held his attention. The Dallas Cowboys are playing the San Francisco 49ers.Garrett doesn't really care for either team, but he sits and watches the game with an enthusiasm, which their marriage lacks.

In order to cover her boredom and sadness, Charley picks up her iPad from the nearby coffee table and logs into Facebook. She sits quietly reading posts from friends about their days—what they had for dinner, what happened at work, what movies they are watching, and who is taking what vacation. Charley sees a post from one of her former classmates, Katherine Hilliard, about a trip she is taking to Australia, and she can't help but comment.

Charlene Morris-Dempsey:
Oh, that's one of my favorite places. I used to fly there regularly when I was a flight attendant right after I graduated from college.

The conversation string begins, and Charley is engrossed as Katherine, asking her for details on more places to go in addition to Sydney, draws her into the discussion further.

The back-and-forth exchange continues as more school friends join in. Suddenly, Peter's name appears in the chat, and Charley's heartbeat accelerates a little as she reads his words.

Peter Pampinelli:
Hey Kate, how is it you are always taking such fabulous vacations, and why can't I come along? And Charlene, you haven't answered me yet ... are you going to be my friend, or what?

Kate and Charlene, their names from high school. Charley is, once again, transported back in time to those formative years in her old hometown.

They weren't bad years, by any stretch of the imagination. They weren't good years either, though. They were just years of growing up and getting ready to take on the real world. High school, for Charley, was a string of years held together by her close group of friends. Charley's secondary school years were just years, nothing special.

Charley thinks about how much she has changed since then. She was quiet, shy, and studious. She didn't say or do much to draw attention to herself. Now, most people consider her a social butterfly. She is always meeting up with her closest friends, and she doesn't have any trouble with being the center of attention. When Charley was in her teens, she was never seen at the keggers the party crowd threw. Now, she and Garrett are always throwing their doors open to friends—inviting everyone over for a cookout is a regular occurrence, especially in the summer when their pool is open and the grill is fired up.

Charley never drank when she was growing up. Now, their wine cellar is fully stocked, and she is rarely without a glass of wine in her hand on the weekends. In high school, Charley felt like she blended into the background. She was neither ugly nor pretty. She hadn't grown into her looks, as her mother so lovingly put it. As Charley got older, her face thinned out, along with her enormous eyebrows revealing her wide-set, deep-blue eyes and her heart-shaped face. Her hair was tamed from a wild mess into a mass of chestnut waves. Now, as opposed to those times long gone by, men and women alike openly admire the smart, confident, sexy woman she presents to the world. The changes didn't come overnight, but rather they were a slow, quiet metamorphosis. Charley worked very hard to change herself, so she could leave behind the ho-hum existence she led back then.

Charley shakes her head to clear the cobwebs of a life she left behind so she can get back into the conversation. She mentally opens a drawer in her head, and stashes all of the feelings of mediocrity she lived with when she was a young teenage girl. She puts back on her present-day, self-assured persona and answers Peter's question in their Facebook conversation.

Charlene Morris-Dempsey:
Well Peter, I haven't had much time to be on Facebook today. I'll gladly accept your friend request now that you've asked me so nicely! ;-)

And with that, Charley presses accept, adding Peter to her list of Facebook friends.

The conversation is flowing, and Charley wants to become more fully engaged, so she logs out of her iPad, gets up from the sofa, and heads to her computer. She continues reading the conversation string with Katherine once she reopens her Facebook wall. It goes back and forth; morphing from Katherine's Australia travel plans to plans to go to the NCAA basketball tournament in New Orleans. Most of her classmates stayed in their little college town and attended school there. For Charley, the thought of staying at home was stifling, so she packed up after graduating and headed out to find her own place in the world—a world far removed from Ann Arbor, Michigan, and the brutally cold winters she faced growing up. As her classmates talk about their travel plans to the tournament, Charley chimes in saying she is so proud of how well their hometown team has played this year and how excited she is for them as they plan their trip down South.

As the virtual conversation goes on, Charley's Facebook message screen pops up.

Peter Pampinelli:
Hey! I just wanted to tell you I'm glad you accepted my friend request. I like that our classmates are all coming back together.

Charlene Morris-Dempsey:
Well, I'm glad you friended me. I really like reconnecting with our class as well, but I have to tell you, I didn't figure you'd remember who I was.

Peter's next words cause a little giggle to escape Charley's lips.

Peter Pampinelli:
Of course, I remember you. You were the one with the dark, frizzy hair and the bushy eyebrows.

With Charley's laugh, Garrett's head cocks to the side, and he asks her what she thinks is so funny. Charley explains to him that one of her old classmates just described what he remembered of her from high school, and it was amusing to her that she would be remembered as the girl with frizzy hair and bushy eyebrows. Garrett's response is nonexistent. He dismisses Charley's laugh, and turns to watch the game.

Charley stays fully engaged in her virtual conversation as her children come in to kiss them goodnight and head up to finish homework. Through her online conversations, she feels vibrant, excited, and happy as Peter teases back and forth with her and the other girls who are chatting happily together and catching up with each other. Charley is still in her virtual world when Garrett tells her he is going up to bed. It is then she decides it is time to rejoin reality and say goodnight to the world of friends on her computer.

Charley and Garrett get ready for bed, side by side. Garrett finishes his nighttime routine, kisses Charley's head, and hops into bed. By the time Charley finishes brushing her teeth, washing her face, and applying her moisturizer Garrett is asleep. Charley quietly shuts off his bedside light and crawls into bed beside him. His breathing is soft and even, but Charley doesn't know whether to believe he is asleep or just faking so he doesn't have to talk to her or, God forbid, possibly be intimate with her.

As Charley lies on her back in their darkened bedroom, her mind starts wandering back to when things started to change between them. And she finds herself face-to-face with her innermost thoughts ... thoughts she has tried to suppress.

* * *

Two words pop into Charley's head, as she thinks about her relationship with Garrett. "You" and "me." In her mind, she begins to examine how they relate to Garrett and her together. In mulling the words over and over, Charley's mind becomes a jumbled mess as she tries to focus on the deep, rhythmic breathing coming from the stillness of her husband next to her. Sleep is too elusive as the words "you" and "me" play over and over and over in her head.

Charley abandons any hope of sleep and ventures back downstairs to hash out her feelings on paper. Ever since she was a little girl, the best way for Charley to deal with her feelings is to write them down, see them on paper, and explore them. She pulls out the journal she keeps for occasions when she needs to vent, and she begins to write.

You and me ... are we in a good spot? I have to say, I think we're not. It's been a hard couple of years, but nothing is going to get better when things are swept under the carpet. Pretenses of everything being fine are there. We're cordial. We kiss. We say please, thank you, and you're welcome. But the reality is, there's so much yuck boiling just under the surface. The life we are living right now seems superficial and shallow, not deep and connected. You and me ... we've gone through a lot. The deep, rich history is there. There is no denying the love is there, too. There is just a lot of work to be done ~ you and me ~ to reconnect. Time must be spent, working, toiling, making things right. Why is there such a void? Why are we not working harder toward reconnecting? Do you even see it? You and me ~ we've been through a lot, and I'm hopeful we'll go through a lot more ~ together ~ always you and me. I'm holding on to hope that there is light ahead where there is now darkness. I'm hopeful we will come out of this together—you and me. I want us to come out stronger. I hope we will. I want to have faith in us—in you and me. Things are always darkest before the dawn, right? You and me. I'm hoping this is the darkest hour before the dawn. I'm hoping dawn comes soon, and we will be strong.

Closing her journal, Charley bows her head, letting the tears slip silently down her cheeks.

* * *

Charley makes her way to bed around 2:30 a.m., after a good cry, pulling herself together, and forcing the sadness to the back of her brain. She falls into a restless, dream-filled world where monsters of despair roam freely, threatening her very existence. In her dream, she tries to run, but her limbs are suddenly leaden. She has lost all control over her muscles. She is frozen in place as the monsters come closer and closer, suffocating her with the feelings of sadness she feels coming from them. It is suddenly hard for her to breathe, and she knows she has to pull herself free from their grip. She wills herself to wake up. Charley claws her way out of her dream, waking with a little yelp.

Her heart rate is accelerated, and her breathing is short and choppy. She looks to her right to see Garrett still sleeping, and her envy is palpable. She wishes she could sleep so soundly and peacefully. Charley looks at the clock on her bedside table to see that it's 6:20 a.m. *Only ten more minutes of sleep.* She knows sleep would be completely elusive at this point, so there is no sense even lying back down.

Oh, well. I might as well make the most of my extra time and get up. She continues her conversation with herself in her head. As her heart rate decreases, and her breathing evens, she swings her legs over the side of her bed and steps into her slippers.

Downstairs, she begins her morning routine. She gets her mug out of the cabinet, pouring herself a generous cup of coffee. She throws in extra sweetener, and as an added bonus, just for this morning, she pours in a generous amount of chocolate and half-and-half to make a mocha coffee. The kids start coming down one by one.

Charley's oldest makes an appearance first. Christina is a stunning beauty. She has all of the grace and charm her mother never had as a junior in high school. She is a decent student with a passion for art that is unrivaled. She already has several colleges looking at her work to showcase within the walls of their academia. Christina greets her mom, as she does every morning, with a cheery "good morning" and a hug. She has always been a morning person and meets each day with a smile on her face. Her teenage years have done nothing to dampen her enthusiasm for life. Christina eats a quick breakfast, kisses her mom good-bye, hops into her convertible red bug and heads to school.

Charley's fourteen-year-old, Noelle, comes down with Andrew. Together, they sit and eat their breakfast, chatting—always chatting—

about school and their mutual friends. Charley is amazed at how well the two get along. She looks at them with softness in her eyes as she listens to their early morning chitchat. With their lunches packed and teeth brushed, they head out the door as their twin brother and sister race down the stairs.

The eight-year-old twins' curly heads appear in the kitchen. Amanda is raring to go to school. The first thing she does is put her lunch in her backpack, makes sure her homework is in its folder, and packs it neatly next to her lunch. Chandler, on the other hand, is a typical eight-year-old boy ... a bundle of energy with no direction. Charley sets aside their breakfast to help get him headed in the right direction—or any direction, just a place where he's not underfoot and irritating the bejeezus out of his twin.

As Chandler and Amanda are finishing their breakfasts, Garrett comes down dressed in scrubs and ready to leave for the hospital. He tells Charley he got a page not long ago that the pace in the ER was picking up. He knows he needs to be there now. A massive accident was just called into the hospital. She watches his instincts as a trauma surgeon kicks him into high gear. He grabs a piece of toast, pours some coffee in a to-go mug, and hugs the kids good-bye. Garrett says a quick good-bye to Charley, chastising her for waking him up when she got out of bed last night. She begins to tell him she couldn't sleep and was trying hard not to disturb him, but she is interrupted by him telling her how poorly he slept because of her constant movement when she came back to bed. *I can't win. I was damned if I got out of bed, and I was damned when I got back into bed.* Her heart constricts knowing she has screwed up, yet again, in Garrett's eyes. She gives him an obligatory kiss on the mouth as he leaves the house and walks to his midnight-blue BMW SUV.

With the twins ready to go, she sends them out the door with hugs, kisses, and lots of love. She watches them as they meander to the bus stop with twenty of their closest friends and neighbors. Charley knows it is safe to close the door on the morning and get to work on her day.

* * *

Charley goes to the kitchen, cleans up from breakfast, and then starts upstairs to her room to make it tidy for the day. After her chores are done, she puts on her running clothes, slips on her running shoes and heads out the door for a mind-clearing run up and down the hilly streets of Louisville, Kentucky.

Charley pounds out five miles in less than thirty-five minutes. She loves to push herself to run faster and faster, throwing sprints in between just for kicks. Most people she knows can't keep up with her, Garrett included, and it is one way she feels strong and powerful. Charley knows it's really not that big of an accomplishment, but she gets a strange satisfaction from it, and she loves the mind-clearing benefits of running the blues away.

Finishing her cool down and walking slowly back into the house, Charley hears her phone ring as she steps into the entry hall. And she does what she has been trained to do since she was a teenager waiting for that all-important phone call from a boy wanting to ask her out—Charley races to the phone to pick it up before the ringing stops. It doesn't matter that now she has caller ID and can return calls quickly, without worrying about who was missed on the phone. This reaction is instilled in her and won't ever be thrown to the wayside. She grabs the phone just as her best friend's number fades to black.

Charley hits redial and is immediately rewarded with Gayle's soothing voice on the other end of the line.

"Hey, do you want to do lunch today?" she asks, with no form of greeting before her question.

"I'd love to! I really need a mental break," Charley responds.

"Wow, you sound drained and down! You can fill me in when we meet. Do you want to meet on Bardstown Road and just let a restaurant choose us?"

It was one of their favorite things to do—wander up and down Bardstown Road, window-shopping and pretending a restaurant picked them. They'd been doing it since they were in college together, and some things, like old traditions between friends, are best when they're not outgrown.

Charley's enthusiastic yes sealed their date, and they planned on lunch at 11:00 a.m.

* * *

Knowing she has two hours before she needs to leave for her lunch, Charley decides to log into Facebook and see what's going on in her virtual world of friends. As her wall lights up with "news" of the day, Charley sees she has a Facebook message from Katherine.

Katherine Hilliard:
Hey!
I was just thinking how much fun it would be if you came to New Orleans for the basketball tournament! I know it's short notice. It's only two weeks away, but there's a group of nine of us going, and I would love for you to come along. Besides, wouldn't it be awesome if Michigan played Louisville?? I think it's a NO-BRAINER!! You need to get yourself to New Orleans!! It's been so long since we've all been back together. It would be like a little reunion. So, look at your calendar, figure it out, and get your ass down to the Big Easy for a shitload of fun!

Oh my gosh, that would be a blast! She pulls out her phone to check her calendar to see what's on the agenda in two weeks. She knows it's not a lot of time to plan, but she would love to make it work. There are a few things on the schedule, but if she starts planning this now, she can get all the gaps covered. She knows Gayle will step in and drive the twins to their events. Charley figures Christina would be more than willing to help shuttle kids from place to place. Since she has gotten her driver's license, Christina loves to get behind the wheel and drive anywhere. She'll run this by Gayle at lunch and then talk to Garrett about it when he gets home from work, hoping that airline tickets aren't too expensive. It could be the one thing that would prevent her from being able to join in the fun. The desire to go is growing stronger and stronger. There is no way she'll pass up this opportunity to reconnect with old friends if she can help it.

As she is drafting her response to Katherine, Peter's name pops up on her screen with a cheery greeting.

Peter Pampinelli:
Hey my sweet, bellissima friend! How are you this morning?

Charley hits reply.

Charlene Morris-Dempsey:
Hey yourself! I'm perfect this morning. I already got in my five-mile run. I have a lunch date planned with my best friend. And now I get a sweet message from an old classmate

Peter Pampinelli:
WOW! It sounds like you have the world at your feet this morning!

Charlene Morris-Dempsey:
Yep, I would say so! :-)

Peter Pampinelli:
I just wanted to tell you how much I like the new picture you put on Facebook yesterday. I didn't want to say anything on your wall, but WOW ... you really do look gorgeous!

Charlene Morris-Dempsey:
That is so sweet of you to say! And with that, I will make it my new profile picture.

Peter Pampinelli:
Good! OK, bella signora, I have to get to work and make some people's dreams come true! Ciao, Bella!

Charlene Morris-Dempsey:
Bye!

With that, Charley logs out of Facebook and heads to the shower so she can primp for her lunch date with Gayle. She gets ready, reveling in the words Peter wrote to her today. He called her "pretty," "gorgeous," and "sweet." She is on cloud nine. Garrett rarely looks her way, and those are words that he hasn't said to her in years. Knowing somebody still finds her attractive at forty-two after having five kids is enough to carry her, happily, through her day.

* * *

Charley's mood is light and cheery when she meets up with Gayle at their favorite shop, The Pink Door Boutique. They can always find unique pieces of clothing and jewelry that make their outfits anything but ordinary. They've also found some duds, but they both love digging through the eclectic items that pass through the store. Charley finds a brooch that she says is "to die for." Gayle takes one look at it and pretends to throw up. It's a giant, overworked piece of plated gold with a fake sapphire set in the middle. Gayle thinks it's hideous and goes on to question her friend's sanity for wanting to buy such an ugly accessory.

Charley isn't hurt by Gayle's critique of her selection. It only makes her want it more. She knows the exact outfit she's going to wear it with the next time they meet. When Gayle sees how perfect it looks on that outfit, she will have to eat her words.

The two friends make their way up to the counter to pay for their purchases.

They stroll out of the store, arm in arm, and the two friends go about their pretense of letting a restaurant pick them. In reality, they both know they're going to end up at the Butterfly Garden Café—it's their favorite place to sit and chat while filling up on fabulous cuisine in a funky, eclectic, but somehow dainty environment.

They make their way into the restaurant and are immediately seated. Both know exactly what they want to eat. Their orders never vary. They usually have the same server, and she always knows what they want. But today, they have a new girl who is obviously in training. Charley has to repeat her order of unsweetened tea, the pear and gorgonzola salad, topped with chicken and the dressing on the side, three times before Trina, their server, finally gets it down. Charley is not sure which part of her order threw Trina more, the fact that she wanted the dressing on the side or the fact that she ordered unsweetened tea. Charley listens as Gayle orders her lunch with ease. As Trina leaves the table, Charley asks, "Why was it so much easier for her to understand your order?"

"Maybe that's because I ordered straight off the menu with no changes. I didn't ask for the Benedictine on the side or unsweetened tea. You know you can't ask for unsweetened tea here and not be met with a bit of a question. Silly girl, we live in the South. Tea is always sweet here." The two old friends share a laugh over Charley's quirky ordering habits and then sit back to chit chat about their kids and their schedules as they wait for their lunches.

When their food arrives Charley and Gayle dig in with gusto. Charley immediately divides it in half, leaving one side completely untouched. Trina returns to the table a short time later to check on Charley and Gayle, asking if everything is OK and makes mention of the fact that Charley doesn't seem to be enjoying her salad because over half is still on her plate. Charley reassures Trina that everything is fine; she's just not that hungry today.

"Oh, don't be offended, Trina," Gayle reassures her, "she never finishes anything on her plate."

Trina says she will box up the remainder of their lunches for them and leaves them to resume chatting.

As soon as Trina leaves the table, Gayle goes in for the kill.

"OK. Charley, spill. What's going on with you? This morning, you sounded sad and dejected, and then when we met at the Pink Door, you looked like the cat that swallowed the canary. You're making me feel like you have two personalities dueling inside that head of yours. Either that, or you've been possessed by aliens who are now controlling your every move—oh, and *now* I understand how you could like such an ugly brooch. You *were* abducted by aliens!"

Charley laughs out loud as Gayle's effusiveness comes barreling out. That's what drew Charley to Gayle, her larger-than-life personality. Gayle takes nothing for granted. She works hard for what she wants and is generous and forgiving to a fault. Gayle rarely has a down day, and if she does, she works hard to focus on the positive and come out on top. Charley loves that about Gayle, and right now, she needs her best friend to hear the story that has been eating at her soul for more than two years. She needs to feel Gayle's effervescence infusing into her to help break the cycle of sadness that is now threatening to swallow every vestige of who she is. By telling Gayle what happened in the past, she will get to eventually morph into the other part of the story—the part that put a smile on her face today.

"OK, you figured it out!" Charley replies. "I was abducted by aliens. They need the brooch for scientific research. It's the blazing stone in the middle. They think it has magical properties, and they want to test it on me. I wasn't supposed to tell anyone about this, but I'll tell them I was tortured so badly by you, I couldn't help but tell."

Now, it's Gayle's turn to laugh. "Oh, Charley. I'm so glad to see you with a genuine smile on your face. It's been gone far too long."

Charley doesn't know what to say. She thought she had done a good job of smiling through the pain, but Gayle had caught on. Charley thought her feelings were hidden fairly well. But then, she remembered this is her best friend ... the one who could see through all of her facades as if she were transparent.

Charley thinks back to how she and Gayle became best friends, nearly instantaneously. It happened when they both showed up at the University of Louisville in their freshman year of college. Gayle was a sweet southern belle from Charlotte, North Carolina, who needed to escape her hometown just as much as Charley needed to escape Ann Arbor, Michigan. While their reasons for leaving their hometowns behind were vastly different, their desire to be in Louisville drew them together. They had been the best of friends ever since.

Charley's mind wanders back to what made her want to leave Ann Arbor so badly. She couldn't handle the suffocation she felt there. Her parents were well known in their small city, and every move Charley made was well documented and reported back to her parents. Charley's dad was a doctor, so people felt obligated to let her parents know what their darling daughter did when she wasn't with them. There were times she felt just like Ariel from the movie *Footloose*. People expected her to behave in a certain way, and when she didn't, it was scandalous. So, she packed up after high school, headed south, and never looked back. Charley adopted Louisville as her own, and it became her home. Gayle's reason for leaving Charlotte was because of an old boyfriend who didn't want to let go. She wanted as much distance between them as possible. She needed to move on, he didn't. He became a creepy stalker. Gayle's family urged to her to look at universities away from Charlotte to help her make a clean break.

Pulling herself out of her reverie, Charley realizes she shouldn't be surprised that Gayle would be the one to see through her facade. They've been together during nearly every phase of life—college students, fresh into the workforce, newly in love, newlywed, new mom. All of the stages they've been through together have helped cement their bond.

And so Charley begins her story, with tears glistening on her lashes. The floodgates open with Gayle's statement that Charley's smile is missing.

"It all started about two years ago, when Garrett's dad died. As you know, Garrett's mom never really liked me or forgave me for marrying her son. She was so angry that we 'had to get married,' in her eyes, anyway. She never listened to me when I told her Garrett had already proposed before I got pregnant with Christina. It just made her more and more angry when I tried to talk to her. Garrett never did much to diffuse the situation between us through the years. He always tried to play himself in the middle, never really wanting to choose sides. And in my eyes, that meant he chose her. I tried so hard, Gayle, to be understanding. I know that he is an only child, and she thinks I 'stole' her right to watch her only son get married. But what she has failed to realize this whole time is that if she had just accepted me and loved me and welcomed me into their family, there never would have been any type of anger. Instead, she let it brew and stew. Gayle, the comments she has made to me over the years are horrendous. And every time, Garrett turns a blind eye, saying that's just how his mom is. I have everything written down. Every mean, snarky, nasty comment she has ever made to me is written down, not to hold onto, but to try and get it out of my system so I don't repeat her meanness. You know how I am, when I get upset, I write, and it calms me down. So, whenever I'm around her, I write."

Charley feels Gayle's penetrating gaze as she finishes her story. "Oh, my sweet, beautiful friend, I wish I had known how terrible things are for you. I knew things were bad, but I had no idea the depth of her vitriol and nastiness. My heart aches for you knowing what I know now," Gayle empathizes.

"She has told me so many times that one particular friend is so much cuter than I am, and if Garrett had any smarts, he would have married her instead of me. That witch even went so far as to say, 'It's too bad Randy is a boy instead of a girl. He's so much cuter than you, Charley. If he had been a girl instead of a boy, Garrett would have married him instead of you.' Gayle, this is Garrett's first cousin! Who the hell says shit like that?" Charley is getting worked up as she talks through what happened, but she can't dwell on those words from the past. She has to move forward to the present.

"When Garrett's dad died two years ago, things got worse," Charley continued. "You were at the funeral, but you missed what happened back at her house afterward. You had already left when Pam lit into me like a piece of kindling. She told me how when I got pregnant with the twins, Garrett went to her and told her he didn't think they were his babies. He'd already had a vasectomy, she said, and there was no way those were his babies growing inside of me. She told me he was sticking with me because of the other kids, but when they were grown and out of the house, he would be gone."

By this time, tears are streaming down Charley's cheeks, and her chin is quivering with every word.

"My heart is breaking for you. This story is killing me. I'm beyond dumbfounded anyone could treat you, my amazing friend, with such contempt. The fact that it's your mother-in-law makes it so much worse. This is the woman who raised the man who promised to love, honor, and cherish you all the days of his life. And that Garrett has done nothing to stop her, makes my blood boil. This is beyond wrong, and something needs to be done to fix it." Charley sees the steely set to Gayle's eyes and knows what is coming next. The questions start coming fast and furious.

"Why the holy hell didn't you tell me all of this before?" Charley sees her anger is getting the better of her, as her nostrils flare in contempt. "OK, I need to settle down a little, or I won't have anything constructive to give you." Gayle takes a deep breath.

Charley begins to explain to Gayle why she didn't tell her anything, and even to her own ears, it sounds trite and dumb. She didn't want Gayle to think badly of Garrett or their marriage. She wanted for everyone to believe the flawless facade they presented to the world. Charley goes on to explain that she didn't want to look like a failure to Gayle, who had the absolute picture-perfect life with a husband who doted on her and their two young sons. He is the ideal man for her best friend, and Charley didn't want anyone, including Gayle, to know that she had anything less than she knew she deserved.

Gayle's next question is obvious, and actually, Charley had expected it first, "Are the twins Garrett's kids? I'm not sure I really needed to ask the question ... "

The tears pool in Charley's eyes as she whispers, "Yes, they are his. I have never, ever cheated on him. His vasectomy was a failure. He didn't go back and get tested twice. Gayle, he knew the babies were his shortly after he told his mom his suspicions. He fessed up to me that he never went back for his rechecks, but he never corrected his mom. She believed for all those years that Amanda and Chandler weren't Garrett's. So when his mom confronted me after the funeral, she still believed it, screaming at me that I was a whore who didn't deserve her son."

"Garrett didn't hear a word of what happened until I told him. By then, his mom was asleep, thanks to her Ambien, and he claimed he couldn't wake her. We left his mother's house and drove home in silence—not because we were grieving for his father, but rather the complete and total lack of respect filled the car. In my eyes, he had failed me, yet again, when it came to his mom. He should have told her what happened as soon as he knew the truth. He should have taken some responsibility for telling his mom the story, and he should have told her to butt the fuck out of our lives a long time ago. But he didn't, and it's put a huge strain on us, on our marriage.

"I don't feel much of anything toward him anymore. I used to want to fight and fix things, but Gayle, it's gotten to be a losing battle. In the past, we would work together to make our relationship the way it was before his mom got so furious with us for getting pregnant and eloping without including her in our plans. She never forgave me and has held a grudge against me all these years. It's impossible to win against a woman like her. I used to wonder how she raised such a sweet, loving man, but sometimes, now, I think he might be more like her than I want to admit. He's aloof to me. He's constantly on his phone when he's home, either texting or playing that stupid Words With Friends game. It seems like he resents my very presence, only acknowledging me when it suits him. He rarely, if ever, looks my way.

Garrett never tells me I'm pretty or beautiful. The sweet name he used for me hasn't crossed his lips in years. He hasn't said 'I love you' in forever. I feel like I am truly invisible to him, like he just wants me to go away. Exactly the way his mom makes me feel, only without her nasty words. It's just gone ... "

Charley's voice trails off, the tears falling silently into her lap as she, for the first time ever, really sees just how bad things are and how little is left.

Gayle interrupts Charley with another question that nearly makes her jump out of her skin.

"Do you think he is having an affair?"

The question had been floating around the periphery of Charley's mind for almost a year now, but she never lets it in. She doesn't want to know the answer, really. She thinks it would kill her to know, even as bad as things are, that Garrett loves someone else.

Charley has always tried so hard to be everything for him, and it would be the end of her if he were having an affair. She knows, deep in her heart, if Garrett were to ever cheat, he would fall in love. Years ago, before they got married, they talked about affairs and love. Garrett told her there would be no way he could cheat. His heart couldn't take it. He couldn't take being in love with two women, he had told her.

Charley confessed that she could probably carry on an affair. She did it in college. She had her boyfriend, and then she had her "romance" on the side. She had been with her boyfriend since high school. He was at one university. She was at another. She loved him, and she didn't want to let him go, just in case he was "the one." Her boyfriend was sweet and nice but a bit boring.

Her romance was just that, a full-blown romance. He was a bad boy, and she had loved it. He was everything her boyfriend wasn't.

She wasn't necessarily proud of her behavior, but she had done it, and no one had gotten hurt. She loved only one, but needed the other, is how she had explained it to Garrett. She knew it wouldn't be like that with Garrett. She would lose him to the other woman, and even as bad as things are right now, her heart still does a little flip-flop, every now and again, when she sees his car pulling into the driveway at night. Her hope is still there that they can weather this storm. Even with all of the bullshit between them, he's still the love of her life.

Charley doesn't want to answer the question, but she does, as honestly as she can.

"I really don't know, Gayle. I really don't think I want to know. As crazy as this sounds, and as much bullshit as there is going on with us, I don't want to think he'd cheat. I think I'd be the one to cheat. I know this sounds crazy. I absolutely know it does, but I meet each and every one of his needs. I can't see how he'd cheat on me."

"*I meet each and every one of his needs.*" Gayle repeats and then goes on to say, "I'm trying to absorb what you just said. How do you meet his needs, my sweet friend?"

Charley reminds Gayle about the couple's retreat she and Garrett went to right after they had Christina. In their encounter, they each learned the five basic needs of a man and the five basic needs of a woman in a marriage.

And Charley tells Gayle she hits every one. "One, I fulfill his needs sexually. He wants it. He gets it. That may be blunt, but it's the truth. Two, I try to get involved in what he likes. I ski with him. I golf with him. I watch football with him."

As Charley sees a smile hinting at the corners of Gayle's mouth she continues, "Seriously, I do try to involve myself in his activities. I might suck at them, but I do try. And three, I have kept myself as attractive as I can, being a forty-two-year-old with five kids. I can still fit in my wedding dress, for Chrissake! Four, I take care of the entire house for him, just as he likes it, and five, I admire the hell out of him, even though he's a shit, sometimes.

"So yes, I try my ass off to fulfill his needs. He, however, falls flat in two of my areas of fulfillment. He never talks to me anymore. It's been shown over and over again that women need conversation to feel connected. And his lack of affection is torture to me. Where I used to get hugs, kisses, and foot rubs, there is now a massive void. Garrett should be quaking in his shoes that I will be the one to find fulfillment elsewhere."

Charley ends with a flourish and a bang of her fist on the table.

Trina comes by to check on them, just as Charley's balled up hand leaves the table. Her face turns bright red at the realization that they are still in the restaurant and surrounded by tables of diners. In telling her tale, Charley lost herself in the story, forgetting they were in a public place. She apologizes to Trina for her outburst, going on to say she needs a glass of pinot grigio. Gayle says, "I second that request, and we'd like to see the dessert menu as well. I figure if we're going to have wine after lunch, we may as well have dessert along with it." Trina takes their order and scurries away, still a little disturbed by Charley's fist banging.

The waitress quickly returns with their wine and the menus, telling them she will be back soon to get their orders. Charley takes a huge gulp out of her generous pour and feels the tension seeping out of her. She's not sure if she's beginning to relax due to the wine or because she has finally shared her story.

"Oh, Love. The transformation of your face is stunning. You look like you just lifted the biggest weight off of your shoulders. I hope sharing your story made you feel a little less alone. You know, you can always tell me anything. We've been friends far too long for you to keep this kind of stuff from me. I'll never, ever judge you." Gayle finishes just as the waitress reappears at their table to take their dessert orders. They both decide on the daily special—molten lava cakes. Charley is feeling beyond decadent. These are two things she never has during the week, wine and dessert. With their orders in hand, the waitress leaves them to their conversation.

"Now that I see your spirit is a little lighter, I want to keep it that way, so let's talk about what made you so happy and smiley this morning, my alien abductee. You were smiling like you had just won the lottery, so you wanna tell me why?"

A delicious little thrill runs through Charley as she remembers the sweet words an old friend wrote to her, and her face lights up like a firefly in July. Thankful for the diversion, she tells Gayle about her conversation.

"Well, I got invited to go to the NCAA basketball tournament by an old high school friend! Who knows, Louisville might be playing Michigan!" Charley begins.

"Oh, really?" Gayle muses, "But let's focus on the invitation for a minute and not the tournament. Who invited you? Peter?"

Charley's face flames bright red, as she answers almost defiantly, "No. It was an old high school friend who happens to be a girl. Thankyouverymuch! Her name is Katherine, and she said there's a whole group of them going down. I'd love to go! I haven't been away from the kids in forever! I'd love to get away and just be me for a little while. I'd love to not have to worry about being 'mom' or 'wife' for a few days. But I haven't talked to Garrett about it, so I really don't know if I'll even be able to go."

Gayle encourages her, "It's awesome to see such excitement on your face. I'll help out however I can. I can take the boys. It's been a while since our boys have been able to get together, so they'll have a blast. And then Garrett would only have to worry about the girls. With Christina driving, it wouldn't be that bad for him."

Charley's excitement builds, thinking she might be able to get away for a while, and her flush grows deeper as she wonders if Peter is going to be at the tournament.

"OK, Missy! What else are you brewing up there in that brain of yours? Your face is bright red. I saw on Facebook that you have a new friend. Could that have anything to do with that massive blush spreading across your cheeks?"

Charley knows it's crazy for a few words from an old classmate to cause such a giddy feeling, but she can't help it. This is Peter Pampinelli, the guy she had a crush on all through high school. Peter Pampinelli, the one who never in a million years looked her way when they were still in school. And now, she has Peter's tantalizing words keeping her company and making her feel so good this morning. It's been such a long time since anyone has looked at her as anything other than Garrett's wife or the Dempsey kids' mom. It just feels good to know someone, somewhere, still thinks of her as a person—and it doesn't hurt that it's Peter making her feel this way.

Charley begins to tell Gayle about the messages from this morning. "Whoa, Charley. Be careful, and remember, men can be shits sometimes. All I have to do is think about how my three brothers treated women at times. I've seen the good, the bad, and the ugly. My alarm bells are ringing right now. Not because I don't think you should be showered with compliments—you should, but maybe not by some guy online. I hate to say this, but you're fairly naïve when it comes to guys. I know they can be charming beyond all belief, but sometimes, they're after something more than you'd think," Gayle warns her.

Laughing it off, Charley replies, "Oh, Gayle ... it was just a little messaging this morning. He was charming and kind, but it's not like he's trying to get in my pants. He was just being nice."

"I'm skeptical. It's just my nature," Gayle explains. "I know it looks like I'm trying to be your protector, and I guess I am, but I need to just step back and be your friend. The smile on your face is what I'm going to focus on, for now. I'll be checking up on you though, Dempsey. Your naïveté brings out the fierce protector in me, my little ingénue."

"Ah, Gayle, you know I love it when you speak French to me, *mon ami. Je suis tres amuse*," Charley says, bringing the conversation back to a less intense level. She doesn't need intense. She needs a break from intense.

"All right, so back to the sweet sixteen tournament. You need to clear this with Garrett, clear your calendar, get ahold of a ticket to the game, book your flight and hotel, and get your ass to N'awlins! It's calling your name! *Now!* So that means we need to get moving so you can get this all done and settled before you chicken out like last time."

"Seriously, Gayle! That was thirteen years ago. Christine and Noelle were babies, and I got sick. I didn't chicken out! I just threw up when we left them, but I still went. I will never live that down, will I?"

"Nope, you'll never live that down for as long as you live. How many other women throw up because they've left their kids at home? The first time I left the boys so Jack and I could reconnect I did a happy dance. I couldn't wait to have him alone, all to myself with his hands roaming all over my body and not worry about a small child bursting in the room asking, 'Daddy, what are you doing to Mommy?' So, our views on that are different! I was ecstatic. You were not! And I think it's hysterical!"

Sighing, Charley looks at her friend whose eyes twinkle mischievously while she tells the story, yet again. Charley can't help but smile and laugh along, herself. She knows she was a little nutso when she left the girls the first time. She didn't do well back then, but she's raring to go now. She needs to get away. She's desperate for a little break.

While they are getting ready to leave, Gayle and Charley realize the waitress never returned with their desserts. Gayle looks at Charley, still with that twinkle in her eye and says, "Wow! You must have really scared her by banging your fist on the table!"

Charley laughs as she signals another waiter so they can get the check. Moments later, their waitress appears, apologizing for forgetting their desserts. She has taken the glass of wine off the bill because of her mistake, she tells them. Gayle lets out a little celebratory "whoop, whoop!" in response to the free drink.

After the waitress leaves, she whispers conspiratorially to Charley as they push back from the table and head out the door, "Maybe next time, we'll get the same waitress, and you can scare her again. Hopefully, she'll give us another free glass of wine."

Shaking her head at her exuberant friend, Charley hugs Gayle good-bye and heads to her car, back to reality.

CHAPTER TWO

CHARLEY RETURNS HOME long before the kids are due in the door and settles down at her computer to get some work done. There are two houses she is currently redecorating. She loves her job and does it fairly well. Charley has built up a decent clientele by word of mouth, by redecorating people's homes with what they currently own to make their living spaces feel fresh and new without breaking the bank. In this shaky economy, more and more people are turning to her services, so she isn't surprised to see three e-mails from prospective clients. Responding to them all, she says she will have time opening up next week as soon as she is finished with her two current houses. From there, she turns her attention to her pickiest client's house and gets to work.

Charley is concentrating on the floor plan and furniture placement in the family room when her Facebook setting notifies her that she has a new message. Her heart skips a beat, wondering if it's Peter. She shakes her head, telling herself to stop acting like a silly, schoolgirl with a massive crush on the senior class president. Charley tries hard to stay focused on the task at hand but eventually loses her battle and opens Facebook to satisfy her curiosity.

Charley's face flushes as she sees the message is Peter's.

Peter Pampinelli:
I'm at my office just after lunch, and I was intrigued enough to prowl through your photos. There are three more pictures of you that are really great. My favorite is the one of you in the big derby hat. It's VERY pretty, chica!

Charley's mouth goes dry at the thought of someone as good-looking as Peter being intrigued enough to want to look through her Facebook pictures. But she puts on her big-girl panties and answers with much more bravado than she feels ...

Charlene Morris-Dempsey:
Ahhh, it can't be considered "prowling" if I put it out there, can it? And you just know how to flatter the ladies, don't you? I'm pretty sure I have reports of you being this suave in high school. I'm glad to know you haven't changed much.

Peter Pampinelli:
I'm not really suave. I just say what I feel. It doesn't always work to my advantage, Bella. And maybe in high school, I was too busy being suave with the wrong girls, which is too bad for me, because you're one extremely sexy signora.

Charley's cheeks burn a little brighter, her heart rate accelerating as she reads and rereads the last line, "... you're one extremely sexy signora."

Nobody, but nobody, had ever called her sexy before. To Charley, those words are reserved for celebrities, not forty-something-year-old moms with five kids. She revels in his flattery, though. It's been so long since Garrett has paid her even the slightest compliment, and she knows for a fact he has never called her sexy. For the first time in a long while, Charley feels desirable. Peter Pampinelli thinks she, Charley, is sexy. Wow!

Play it cool, Charley. Play it cool. You want to keep being told you're gorgeous and sexy—don't blow this! Taking a deep breath, she begins to type her response.

Charlene Morris-Dempsey:
Nope, you're seriously suave ... you make people feel good! Thanks for all of your kind words—you make my day whenever I see your comments! As far as high school goes, I was just a little too shy and wallflower-ish for you to notice! :-/ I have to say, your wife has to be on cloud nine getting all of your fabulous compliments! And I say, "Good for you," for saying what

you're thinking. I'm not a good "player," either (my filter is broken ... I say what's on my mind, too!)

Peter Pampinelli:
A player? That doesn't sound good. I know you were quiet and shy in high school, but we're not in high school anymore. We're all grown up, so it's impossible for me not to notice you now. How about that?

Charley's breath catches in her throat as she reads "... it's impossible for me not to notice you now." She takes a minute to compose herself and begins to reply.

Charlene Morris-Dempsey:
See ... told you my filter is broken. I didn't mean YOU were (or are) a player! Just meant it's good to say what's really on your mind! I like that in a person! And glad to know I'm not ignorable now! You're a fantastic friend to have!

Peter Pampinelli:
I know you didn't mean I was a player, but I'm having some fun with it! And I like the "You're a fantastic friend to have."

With Peter's last response, Charley begins to relax and enjoy herself in the conversation, which is making her feel alive and vibrant. Her response comes a little more easily this time.

Charlene Morris-Dempsey:
Have fun with it, Skippy! Paybacks are hell! ;-)

It seems to take forever for Peter to respond, and Charley begins to wonder if she crossed some sort of imaginary line when his response finally comes through.

Peter Pampinelli:
I just finished talking to Katherine. She told me you're thinking of joining us in the Big Easy for the tourney! Is that true? I would love for you to come!

Holy shit! He's going to the basketball tournament?

She could see him, live and in person. She could hear him say she was gorgeous! How much fun would that be?

A small voice in the back of her head admonishes, *Oh my God, Charley! Calm down! You are a grown woman, not a silly, little teenage girl! Get a grip on yourself!*

Charley shakes her head, essentially clearing it from the stupid thoughts coursing through her mind and steadies her fingers, getting ready to reply.

Charlene Morris-Dempsey:
I had no idea you were going! That would be GREAT! I still have to get the go-ahead from my husband and make sure I have all the kids' activities taken care of, so I'm still in the preplanning stage. But I think it would be a blast!

Peter Pampinelli:
Well, I have an extra ticket with your name on it, so you better get your pretty little ass down to N'awlins!

Charley nearly falls off her chair when his reply comes through. His phrase "pretty little ass" just about knocks her, literally, on said ass. Charley gathers her wits about her and starts typing, putting on a facade she is not sure she could continue if she actually did go to New Orleans.

Charlene Morris-Dempsey:
Well, Mr. Pampinelli, that was mighty sweet of you, but you haven't seen my ass, so how do you know if it's pretty or not?

With her heart beating fast in her chest, Charley hits send before she has a chance to chicken out.

Peter Pampinelli:
Oh, Bella, by the looks of you, how could your ass not be pretty, little bellissima signora?

Oh, dear! Did Charley read that right? This was almost too much for her. To go from zero attention from her husband to having a hot high school classmate saying sweet words to her, is almost more than she can handle. All she can manage with her reply is:

Charlene Morris-Dempsey:
Wow!

Sitting with her head in her hands for a few minutes, she lets her heartbeat settle down. Charley knows she needs to get back to work, but this is so much more fun.

Peter Pampinelli:
All right, bellissima signora. I need to get back to work. I enjoyed our chat immensely. Ciao, Bella!

Charlene Morris-Dempsey:
Bye!

With that, and a smile on her face, she logs out of Facebook and tries to collect her wits before Christina is due home in fifteen minutes.

* * *

He will have her in his collection soon. He knows it.

But in the meantime, his needs are begging for release. He pulls up his picture gallery on his desktop. He locks his office door and lowers the blinds. He calls his secretary to tell her he is not to be disturbed for an hour or so. He had a rough night with his wife, he says. She was up and down all night with nightmares. His secretary knows about his wife's accident and how dependent she is on him. "You are a saint," Peter's secretary says, "I promise to keep everyone at bay, so you can have a little nap." With that, his quest begins for the one who will satisfy him this afternoon.

Ahhh, there she is. She's the one I need today, he thinks to himself, looking at her photo on his computer. He pulls out his phone and dials her number.

"Hey, I have my afternoon free, and it has your name written all over it."

"Fabulous. I need a good Skype fuck," she says.

Moments later, they are face-to-face on Skype, for their virtual sexual encounter, and the verbal build-up begins. He tells her how he wants to take his tongue and run it up and down the length of her body, stopping at all of the tender places he has visited during the few times they have been together. He goes on to tell her that he is hungering for her sweet, wet warmth, and he wants to tease her slowly with the tip of his tongue by flicking licking lightly over her sensitive areas as she approaches her climax.

His voice is low and slow as he continues to describe in great detail how he would arouse her if they were together. He watches her head tilt backward when she brings out her Mighty Butterfly. He is building her up to a climax with his voice, and he derives a satisfying thrill knowing she is helping herself continue on her path of bliss. He watches her eyes close, and her head rolls back as he tells her to lower the camera. He wants to watch her come, he says. She does as he directs, and he feels the pull of her orgasm coming faster and faster. He knows the thought of being on camera for him increases the desire of her release, and he watches as she careens over the precipice of gratification. As he watches the pleasure course through her body, he knows she is fully engaged in her own sensations. He is quietly taking pictures of her with her head tipped back, mouth open, rapture over her face, and her legs spread open.

He is rock hard from her image on the screen in front of him, and now it is his turn to be taken over the edge; she will tell him exactly what she wants to do to him. His needs are kinkier than hers, so for him, she talks about spanking, blindfolding, and binding his legs and one arm so he is at her mercy. She tells him to take his free hand and begin to allow his release. He comes quickly. Their sexual needs met, for the time being, they say their farewells and each go back to their reality. Sexual fantasy time is over.

* * *

Garrett comes home from work, pleasantly surprised to find Charley sitting at the kitchen counter working on her laptop. Usually, she only works in her sunshine-filled office just off of their bedroom where she closes the door to make sure he or one of the kids does not disturb her. Garrett greets her with a small kiss on the cheek, and he notices the table is set for dinner, and glasses of his favorite cabernet, Caymus, are poured for them both.

Garrett is happily surprised by all of the differences tonight. There are no children around. The house is quiet. Charley tells him that his favorite restaurant, Cafe Lou Lou, is delivering three orders of pasta Bolognese and three muffaletta sandwiches for dinner, along with salads and fresh, hot bread. Garrett's mouth is watering at the thought of his favorite dinner being delivered shortly, but he can hardly contain his shock at the vast difference in Charley tonight. She never has wine on a weekday, and Cafe Lou Lou is not on her menu for anything less than a special occasion. Garrett doesn't want to spoil the evening by pointing out these differences to Charley, so he focuses on enjoying it.

He sits down next to Charley at their kitchen island and breathes in the aroma of the wine. He loves the flavors of the big, rich, fruity cab. It's such a well-balanced wine. Garrett can think of no other that matches it. He takes a small sip, savoring the flavors as he looks over at Charley's laptop. She is perusing Delta.com, and Garrett's curiosity overcomes him as he asks, "What are you doing?"

Garrett watches Charley pick up her glass of wine and swirl the dark, rich liquid as she begins to explain her invitation to the NCAA tournament. Garrett notices the soft flush on her cheeks and hears the excitement in her voice as she talks about meeting up with old friends she hasn't seen in years. Charley says, "Garrett, Louisville may end up playing Michigan, and I think it would be a blast to see both my hometown and my adopted town's teams face off against each other." Garrett can't help but smile at his wife of sixteen years as her excitement bubbles over. He hasn't seen her this happy in quite some time. Lately, she's been very quiet and withdrawn. She rarely smiles at him, and her sense of humor seems to have vanished.

With all of these things in mind, and seeing the smile on her face, he turns to her and offers, "Tell me what I need to do to help you go."

Charley explains to Garret she already has most of the details covered and organized, going on to explain that Gayle said she would take the boys for the weekend.

Garrett listens to Charley as she lays out the few things he would have to be responsible for in the three days she would be gone, and with that, he picks up his glass of wine and exclaims, "Here's to basketball! Go Blue! Or wait, should I say 'Go Cards?' "

Charley raises her glass as well, and they toast to a trip south.

Garrett sits with Charley as she looks for plane tickets. "I know the expense of a plane ticket would be a big deterrent. I'm hoping prices aren't too high right now, even though we're only two weeks out. Sometimes, I really miss flying. A non-rev ticket would be sweet right about now."

"If the prices are too high, do you think one of your friends who are still flight attendants could hook you up with a buddy pass?"

"I guess I could, but it's a big risk. And I don't know if it would be worth it, just in case I got bumped over and over. But hey ... look at that, a round-trip ticket to New Orleans on Delta—$199. That's not too bad," she declares as she looks over at Garrett.

"Nope. Not too bad at all. I say, book it and go."

With her tickets secured, Charley messages Katherine and tells her she has her flight booked and is ready to for an adventure-filled weekend.

Katherine's response is immediate.

Katherine Hilliard:
OMG, I cannot wait! That is awesome! Don't worry about a hotel. We already have a block of rooms at the Hotel Monteleone. You can just share with me—I don't have a roommate yet! This is going to be a blast!"

Charley does a little happy dance, and Garrett smiles. He can't believe all it took to see her this happy was a plane ticket and a basketball game.

They sit together for a while longer. Garrett tells an enthusiastic Charley about his day, and for the first time in a long while, she sits and listens—asking questions and being involved. He can't believe his luck this evening. His favorite wine, his favorite meal, and now the lively, bubbly Charley he used to know sitting with him. Talking.

All too soon the doorbell rings with dinner, and the kids take that as their cue to come bursting forth from upstairs. What Garrett didn't know was Charley had asked them to stay in their rooms for a while so she could talk to their dad. It rarely happens that they are shooed away for an adult conversation, so they acquiesced easily, staying put for a little bit. The kids are all bundles of energy as they come pouring into their cozy and inviting kitchen. It is the heart of their house. Each child prefers to stay underfoot, getting their homework done in the warmth of the kitchen rather than going to their rooms when they get home from school. Garrett knows Charley loves the hustle and bustle of a busy kitchen, and that's why she never sends them away. And usually, he loves the big, sunny kitchen to be full of children and noise, but right now, he would love to have the quiet time he had with Charley back, just for a few more minutes.

After dinner is done and the kids are cleaning the kitchen, Garrett tells Charley how much he enjoyed their few minutes alone.

"It's been a long time since I've seen you this happy. I'm glad you're going to get away for a few days," he says. "It'll be good for you, and maybe this time, you won't throw up."

They both laugh at the shared memory, but what Garrett doesn't know is that a little pang of guilt hits Charley. He has no idea part of the reason she is so happy is because Peter is going to be there.

* * *

Charley takes a deep gulp of air as she turns to head up the stairs. The pang of guilt she had when she was with Garrett grows into a sharp stab. She is excited to be going away, excited to reconnect with old friends and to see Peter in person, but part of her, deep down inside, tells her this is not a good idea. The voices in her head go to war over Peter and Garrett.

Peter is paying attention to you and calling you sweet names, and Garrett can't even spare a glance your way. It's not like you're having an affair, you're just enjoying a little attention.

Yes, but Garrett was so sweet tonight. He was kind and funny and so willing to let me go.

Oh, darling, have you forgotten how much he's been ignoring you? You deserve a little attention.

Charley shakes her head to clear out the voices and tells Garrett over her shoulder she enjoyed their time, too. Part of her wishes so hard he would sweep her off her feet and take a weekend away so they could keep reconnecting, but she knows that won't happen. He hasn't asked her to do anything together in more than a year. Whenever she proposes a date or time together, Garrett always has something else planned—a fishing trip, a guys' weekend, a concert, work … time together never seems to materialize when Charley suggests it. It's disheartening to always be rejected, so she stopped asking. A little knot of sadness wells up in her chest as she relives the few minutes spent at the kitchen counter, wondering why days couldn't always be like this. Time together would be the balm her wounded soul needs. Her eyes are awash in conflicting emotions as she walks back to Garrett and places her hand on his cheek.

* * *

With her laptop in hand, Charley heads up to her office and closes the door behind her so she can work on her client's house. She sits down at her desk, opens the file on the house, and begins to work. She is so engrossed in the job at hand that she fails to notice her Facebook notification until nearly an hour has passed, and she sees the flashing icon at the top of her screen.

Her heart does a crazy little beat when she realizes it's Peter. Her bitchy inner voice comes back with temptation; *You deserve a little positive attention. Open it!*

She opens his message with far more bravado than in past days and reads his words. A smile spreads across her face.

Peter Pampinelli:
Buona sera, Bella. (In case you didn't know, that's Italian for "Good evening, beautiful"). This is "Skippy." How are you tonight?

Charlene Morris-Dempsey:
Hello to you and THANK YOU. That is so sweet of you to say. I am just trying to finish up a house for a client. She's very picky. I've done and redone work for her before. It's painful, but she pays well.

Peter Pampinelli:
What do you do, tesora?

Charlene Morris-Dempsey:
I "create beautiful spaces in ordinary places." At least that's what my business cards say I do.

Peter Pampinelli:
Hmm ... Sounds like that would be an easy job for you. You could do that just by walking in a room. But please explain it for me.

Charley's heart nearly stops beating. She's sure she's hallucinating, and those words really aren't there, and if they are, they certainly aren't meant for her. Charley shakes her head and refocuses ... they are still there, and they are written to her. *Wow!* She is blown away that anyone would say that she could make a room beautiful by walking into it. Taking a deep breath, Charley responds as casually as she can.

Charlene Morris-Dempsey:
Why thank you, kind sir. How very debonair! My actual job is to "redecorate" people's homes with stuff they already have. I take a room and make it new and fresh by repurposing things from other areas of their house and by digging up old odds and ends in their attic. Sometimes, they give me a budget to add extras in here and there, but mostly I try to work with what they have.

Peter Pampinelli:
Just speaking the truth. And your job sounds like it would be very interesting and entertaining—digging through people's attics, seeing what they don't really want anymore but don't have the heart to discard.

And debonair, huh? I have to be honest. I don't think I was very debonair earlier when I made the ladies on my office staff eat Pies 'n' Thighs' donuts. What do you think?

Charlene Morris-Dempsey:
Are you KIDDING? Of course it's debonair! And I don't think "forced" would be the word I would use when it comes to those ... I would pay big money to eat donuts from Pies 'n' Thighs!

Peter Pampinelli:
And just for the record, I did not "force." I justified, that's what I did. And since you know of Pies 'n' Thighs, I guess that means you've been to New York City?

Charlene Morris-Dempsey:
It's one of my favorite places ... EVER! Both New York City and Pies 'n' Thighs. So now it's my turn to ask ... what do YOU do?

Peter Pampinelli:
I have a publishing firm here in the city.

Charlene Morris-Dempsey:
How cool is that!

Peter Pampinelli:
The next time you're here, you should let me know. We'll go tour the city together. On a different note, I have to tell you these messages have your gorgeous, new profile picture attached. I just looked up from typing, and it looks like you are staring directly at me, with your beautiful blue eyes saying, "You are SUCH a dork!"

All Charley can do is take a deep breath at the "tour the city together" comment and laugh out loud at the thought of anyone thinking Peter could be anything close to a dork.

Charlene Morris-Dempsey:
LOL ... most people say I'm the dork!

Peter Pampinelli:
Ah, my dolce friend. It's time for me to go. It was wonderful chatting with you tonight, and I can't wait to talk again soon. Ciao, Bella. And don't forget I think you're beautiful.

Charlene Morris-Dempsey:
Thanks. I needed that more than you know!

Peter Pampinelli:
Ignore me. I'm just pining out loud a bit ... I will be better soon.

Charlene Morris-Dempsey:
Pining, Skippy? Really? Seriously—pining? You crack me up! You only see the "good" me—my makeup and hair done with a good smile ... smoke and mirrors, babe, smoke and mirrors. I'm grumpy sometimes. I have some gray hair and some wrinkles. That's the real me. You are one of a kind, saying you're pining!

Peter Pampinelli:
Yes. You are 42. You are going to have all of those things.

Charlene Morris-Dempsey:
I do. I'm not worried about it. I'm just stating facts.

Peter Pampinelli:
I'm still going to pine a bit, OK?

Charlene Morris-Dempsey:
You, my friend, are a flirt. Pine away ... goodnight.

Peter Pampinelli:
Ah ... thank you, I will! Ciao, Bella!

Charley's heart is light, and a smile plays across her lips as she reads and rereads the messages between them. She is shocked that Peter would think she, Charlene Morris—the girl with the frizzy dark hair and bushy eyebrows from high school—is beautiful. But it must be true, since it's written down in black and white for the entire world to see.

Oh shit! It's written down for the entire world to see, including Garrett. What the hell would he think if he saw all of these messages? *Holy crap,* Charley thinks to herself, as she looks back on the entire thread of their conversation and tries to decide what to do. Delete all? Delete some? Which of those options makes her seem less guilty?

Oh, Charley! her little voice chides. *There's nothing there. Just a guy telling you that he thinks you're beautiful. Nothing else. There is no reason to worry about these messages. They are nothing.*

Charley tries to ease her conscience by listening to the little voice in her head. *There is nothing to worry about,* she thinks to herself. *They are just words. That's all. Nothing more, nothing less.*

CHAPTER THREE

SHE MAKES HIM so horny. Her beauty drew him in, as is always the case when he is looking to add to his collection, but as he's gotten to know her, her naïveté combined with her sense of humor, wit, and charm shows him she is something a little special. He can tell she has no idea where all of this is heading. He prefers it that way. He likes keeping the element of surprise on his side. He is in her albums on Facebook now, looking through her pictures and finding the ones that show her body clearly. He stops at the images of her at the beach in her tiny bikini. She is perfectly toned and beautiful. He feels such a rush of desire when he looks through her photos, but he needs to control himself or he'll spook her away. She's skittish and needs careful handling. But right now, he needs relief from the familiar tightening in his pants.

Hmm … He thinks to himself, as he sits in his home office with the door locked. Who should it be tonight? He scrolls through his photo gallery. There she is, the one for tonight. She is the one who needs to help him find relief. He is looking at a picture of her naked on her back. Her breasts are round and firm, nipples hard, her legs are spread with her toy inside her. Her glazed eyes are directed at the camera; she has just thoroughly enjoyed a massive orgasm. He was her photographer, and he remembers the night quite clearly. His pants become tighter as he sinks back into the memory of her. After she pleasured herself with her vibrator, she turned over on her stomach to give him access to her backside. Her second orgasm was just as intense as her first, as he ejaculated into her. She is the one who needs to satisfy him tonight. He hears a light tap at his office door.

"Fuck," he swears to himself.

His erection fades just a little as he answers the knock with his voice. His wife tells him she hears a noise in the house. She's scared and thinks there might be an intruder or a fire. She does this often—hears things where there is no noise. Ever since her accident, she's become paranoid and afraid. She has a nurse while he's at work, but she leaves at seven o'clock on the button. Working with Beth is one of the hardest jobs there is. She has the mental capacity of a seven-year-old who distrusts everyone, and when she gets agitated, there is no reasoning with her.

Her nurse is a saint, in his eyes. He can barely tolerate his wife's presence, but he took his vows ten years ago and plans to honor them. He told the world he'd be by her side for better or for worse, in sickness and in health, for richer and for poorer, as long as they both shall live. These vows, along with his signature on the prenuptial agreement, are the ties that bind. He is stuck, and he knows it. He rises and goes to soothe his wife. But first he needs to calm his erection, fully. His urges are pressing, straining hard against the fabric of his pants. His erections scare her. She no longer understands the pleasures between a man and a woman. She screams every time she sees his erect penis, so he tries hard to hide all forms of sexuality from her. Hopefully, he can come back into his home sanctuary when, or if, he gets her settled.

* * *

Charley rolls easily out of bed the next morning, feeling a smile creep across her face as she remembers that Peter thinks she's beautiful. She can't remember if Garrett has ever told her that, and if he has, it hasn't been in years. Charley wonders, for the hundredth time, why she and Garrett have let their marriage fall into such disrepair. Why can't he see that all it takes is a little attention, a kind word, a look, or a touch? But right now, there's nothing.

Except last night in the kitchen, the little voice in the back of her head chides, reminding Charley, *you did a little work for him, and look how nice your time was.* Her smile falters as her conscience roars inside her brain.

The morning routine runs smoothly, and the kids get out the door with ease. Charley sends Garrett off to work with a hug and a kiss. As the door closes behind him, Charley goes to her computer, conflicted. She's hoping there's a message, yet feels guilty at the same time, too. She does her morning scroll through Facebook, commenting here and there. Charley updates her status and waits a little bit to see if Peter will message her this morning. After about half an hour of pretending to work while waiting for a message, Charley shakes her head at her own idiocy and logs out of Facebook to get away from her virtual world and back into reality.

Her phone buzzes with a text message from Gayle, forcing Charley to realize how much she has accomplished since she sat down to work.

10:53 a.m.
Hey! Just checking in this morning! Are you headed to New Orleans?

Charley's response is immediate and enthusiastic.

10:53 a.m.
YES! Garrett was so excited for me to be able to go. And yes, he brought up the puking incident from last time, too. :-P

Charley's phone rings before she has a chance to hit reply. She can hear Gayle's excitement on the other end of the line.

"Hey, Friend! I'm so happy you are going."

"I can't believe it, Gayle," Charley says. "I can't believe I am so excited to be going to watch basketball!"

Charley can feel Gayle's delight through the phone, and they begin to talk about the kids and the logistics of the weekend. Charley's flight leaves on Wednesday, the game is on Friday, and she comes home Saturday night. Gayle says, "Charley, you will have three nights to party and enjoy yourself without thoughts of home and family. I got you covered."

Charley knows Gayle has been to New Orleans quite a few times with her husband, and she knows she's dying to impart her knowledge on the places to stay and the places to avoid.

"Where are you staying?" Gayle asks.

Charley stops for a minute, trying to remember. "It's the Hotel Monteleone. I'm not sure exactly where it is, but Katherine told me I could share a room with her, so that will be good. I'll get to spend time with her! I haven't seen her in forever, and I'm really looking forward to getting to have her all to myself."

"Oh, I love the Hotel Monteleone. Jack and I have stayed there once or twice. You'll love it. It's in just the right spot, and you should be able to walk to the Superdome for the game. Which reminds me, did you get a ticket? I hear they're nearly impossible to get."

A small flush brightens Charley's cheeks, and she is thankful her friend is not sitting across from her as she answers. "Yes, I was told I have a ticket as long as I get myself down to New Orleans." Charley's flush becomes even deeper as she remembers that Peter told her to get her "pretty little ass to N'awlins."

"How, pray tell, did you end up getting a ticket so fast?" Gayle wants to know.

The words come tumbling out of Charley's mouth before she has a chance to stop them, "Peter says he has one for me."

Charley senses Gayle's disapproval, and before she has a chance to voice anything, she heads her off at the pass, "Gayle, I'm going to pay him for the ticket, so don't worry about him having ulterior motives. It's fine. I promise."

Charley can tell Gayle is somewhat appeased at her assurance that she will take care of her own ticket, so the matter is dropped, and instead, she questions Charley about who else is going.

After the Facebook chats back and forth with Katherine, Charley is pretty sure she knows who is going, and she goes on to list the group she thinks will be there.

Gayle says, laughing, "Wow, that's quite a list! And did you realize it's you, about six other girls, Peter and only one other guy? Those two guys are gonna have quite the time keeping all you women in line."

Gayle and Charley talk a while longer about the upcoming weekend, making sure they're organized so it runs seamlessly for everyone. After they're fairly certain they have all of their bases covered, Charley says good-bye, and the two friends hang up.

* * *

After hanging up with Gayle, Charley logs into Facebook. She wants to ask Peter if he really has a ticket for her. And, more importantly, she wants to make sure he knows she intends to pay for it. And that's when she sees the message from him, one he sent while she was offline.

Peter Pampinelli:
Bella signora! How are you this morning? I was just thinking about you. I have to tell you I'm really enjoying our conversations and getting to know you better. I kind of screwed up in high school ... I could have been with the prettiest girl in the whole school, instead, I was busy chasing the wrong kind.
I'm still pining, I guess.

Charley's heart is racing. Seriously, are these words for her? Peter is still pining? Pining for her?

Charlene Morris-Dempsey:
Why, Mr. Pampinelli, how very sweet of you to say. I'm flattered, you flirt.

Charley knows she should walk away. She knows she should close the door on this flirtation, but it felt so good to have someone paying attention to her and telling her she's pretty and beautiful.

Peter Pampinelli:
Yes, I am a flirt, and I am thoroughly enjoying flirting with you. You're adorable. Your beauty and charm are going to be my downfall.

Holy cow. Is this the same guy she went to high school with? The same one she had such a crush on? And here he is writing sweet words to her. Little alarm bells start going off at the back of her brain, but the heady feeling of lavish attention quickly stops them from clanging.

Charlene Morris-Dempsey:
I don't think I've ever known anyone quite like you before.

Peter Pampinelli:
I want to keep these messages going between us because I love looking up at my computer and seeing your alluring eyes staring back at me.

As much as Charley wants to keep seeing these flattering words come up on her screen, she knows she needs to make sure the boundaries are set, so she tries to deflect with some humor.

Charlene Morris-Dempsey*:*
GULP! You really know how to get to a girl, huh?

Peter Pampinelli:
I'm just telling it like I see it. Your eyes are gorgeous, as is the rest of you. I can't wait to see you in person. I think New Orleans is going to be something special.

Little butterflies start stirring around in Charley's stomach, and she can't help but feel more than flattered at his pretty words. His flattery is going to be her undoing.

Peter Pampinelli:
I have a secret for you … Do you think you can keep it?

Her breath catches, as she wonders what kind of a secret Peter would have for her.

Charlene Morris-Dempsey:
Yes, I think so. As long as you're not going to tell me you're a mass murderer or a crazy psychopath. I'm enjoying getting to know you, so I don't want to ruin it with bad news like that.

Charley is pretty proud of her response, considering her nerves have taken over, wondering what his secret is.
Time ticks by as she waits for his reply. The wait is nearly unbearable, so she turns her attention to where it should be—work.

VIRTUAL LIES 57

* * *

Her:
Hey you! I saw you were online and wanted to show you this picture. Check Snapchat!

Him:
Oh, baby, I can't wait to see what you have for me today.

Her:
I got a new hairstyle and wanted to share it with you!

He knows what kind of a hairstyle she wants to show him. He knows her well by now. She has been a part of his collection for years, and he loves the pictures she sends. The camera does not inhibit her. She seems to be freed by having her most private parts photographed. Her face is never seen in her photos; maybe that's why it's so liberating for her. She is one of his favorites. She's not demanding or greedy. She knows the rules. She follows them and is well rewarded not only for her compliance but also her enthusiasm. He quickly pulls up Snapchat on his iPhone and opens her picture. Before it has a chance to disappear, he takes a photo of it. He wants to be able to view this one over and over.

Her:
I see you took a screenshot of my picture. You are terrible. I use Snapchat for a reason, you know. I like the whole notion of the "self-destruction" of the photos after nine seconds, and you know that, you little stinker.

Him:
Oh, darling, you know I like to keep looking at your photos over and over. You have the most artistic way of displaying your wanton womanly ways. I have to say, you have outdone yourself with this one. The arrow is pointing the way to the exact place I want to visit. You look all moist and warm below that arrow, and I just want to make you come. Now. FaceTime.

Her:

I can't FaceTime now. My husband is due home soon. Just talk me through it. Tell me what you want to do to me.

Him:

I want to take my fingers and run them lightly around your wetness.

Her:

Mmm ... keep going.

Him:

I want to take my tongue and follow the path of my fingers. If I were with you right now, I would take the tip of my tongue and make it flat against your clit. Then I would move lower and turn my tongue into a point, lightly licking away your juices.

Her:

Oh, God! That sounds so good! I want more! Please!

Him:

I want you to come. Now. Take your fingers and trace all of those parts I just told you I wanted to trace. Do everything I just told you. Now, insert your fingers and swirl them around inside of yourself. Imagine those fingers are me inside of you, just like when we were together last time. Remember how I felt moving slowly in and out of you until you came so hard while my thrusts got harder and harder. I am ready to come with you now. My hand is on my shaft, and I am remembering. I am almost there. Come with me. NOW!

Her:

Oh my God!

Him:

God, your picture turned me on. Show me more now. I want to see you now that you have had your orgasm. Show me how wet you are for me.

Her:
Mmm ... give me a minute.

He knows the picture will arrive. He can't wait to see her newest photo. He wants to see how red and relaxed her pussy is after her release. Where it was engorged and ready for sexual pleasure earlier, it should be soft and pliant now.

Him:
Where is my picture? I want to see you.

Her:
It's taken and sent.

Him:
God, I love your money shot, honey. That is beautiful. And it's made even better knowing it was taken just for me. I need to get back to work, tesora.

Her:
I do, too. I'll Snapchat you later. :-) That was an awesome release for me.

* * *

Peter Pampinelli:
Hey, bella signora! Sorry about the delay. I was on the phone with a highly excitable author whose ruffled feathers needed to be soothed.

Charlene Morris-Dempsey:
Oh my gosh. Don't worry about it at all.

Charley is trying hard to play it cool. Even though she understands how work is, she did get a little worried. But she'd never let on to Peter. She needs him to think she is as self-confident as she portrays herself online. In fact, she reminds herself, she had better get used to acting more confident if she's going to see him in a little more than two weeks. All of these thoughts go tumbling through Charley's head as she presses send.

Peter Pampinelli:
Back to my secret ... do you want to hear it?

Charley's heart races a little, wondering what kind of a secret a guy like him could have for a girl like her.

Charlene Morris-Dempsey:
Absolutely.

Her armpits are sweaty, and her cheeks are flushed as she waits for his reply.

Peter Pampinelli:
I had the biggest crush on you in high school. I was just too shy to tell you.

Charley's mind goes blank. Of all the things she expected from Peter, that wasn't it. Maybe she had wished for it, or had hoped for it in the deep, dark recesses of her brain, but never would these thoughts ever be anywhere near the forefront of her consciousness. With no idea how to respond, and completely and totally at a loss for words, Charley tries hard to come up with something witty in response, but there's nothing. Not. One. Damn. Thing.

And then Charley reminds herself that she is a married woman with five kids. High school was years ago. *His secret shouldn't affect her like this.*

Her mind starts to wander to her present-day world. Life with Garrett is so unfulfilling. Their sex life is nonexistent. Garrett never makes passes at her. She tries so hard to keep herself trim. She knows she's not the same woman she was seventeen years ago when she and Garrett met, but there are reasons ... five of them. Her body shifted and changed with each pregnancy. But at least she tries to stay in shape and slim. She watches what she eats, and she exercises like crazy to keep unwanted pounds at bay. Food she would love to eat rarely passes her lips so she doesn't get too heavy. There is no bacon or cookies or candy in her diet. She drinks her coffee black so she can save calories. She only drinks wine on the weekends, saving up her calories during the week so she can splurge. When she was younger, and perhaps thinner, Garrett couldn't keep his hands off of her, but now, there is nothing. No contact. He would rather watch TV than be intimate with her.

Her romantic world is gone. Garrett used to write her sweet notes and leave them on the counter for her when he would go away for a conference or a guys' getaway. Those are long gone. There are no compliments or pretty words for her from him. Romance is no more.

Her mind comes back to the present as her computer dings.

Peter Pampinelli:
Hello!?! Are you there? Did I scare you off?

Charley responds quickly and honestly.

Charlene Morris-Dempsey:
Yes, I'm here. And no, you didn't scare me off. I'm just trying to figure out how to respond. I don't normally have guys telling me they used to have crushes on me.

Collecting herself a little, Charley finishes her thought.

Charlene Morris-Dempsey:
At least that's a "used to have the biggest crush on you in high school!" LOL.

Peter Pampinelli:
I'm going to be completely honest. It's not a "used to." I still do. I can't get you out of my mind. I looked at your pictures again and saw the one of you with your kids at the beach. You are one bellissima mamma. You had on that bikini, and you are stunning.

Charley's jaw drops as her heartbeat accelerates. But she responds candidly and quickly before her courage fails her.

Charlene Morris-Dempsey:
Oh my. This is getting dangerous for me, Peter. Things between my husband and me aren't so great right now, and your sweet words are wreaking havoc on my brain.

Charley can feel Peter's smile across the miles with his response.

Peter Pampinelli:
Ah, Bella! I am so enjoying getting to know my beautiful high school classmate. You are one of a kind, and your eyes mesmerize me when I see your messages pop up on Facebook. I'd love to get to know you a little better. Enjoy me. Enjoy my words and my flirting. I want to enjoy you, too.

Charlene Morris-Dempsey:
Ummmm ... I don't know. I haven't done anything remotely close to flirting with somebody else, online or in person.

Peter Pampinelli:
It's OK if you don't want to. We will always be friends.

Charlene Morris-Dempsey:
Can I ask you a question?

Peter Pampinelli:
You're going to ask me about my marriage, aren't you?

Charlene Morris-Dempsey:
Yes.

Peter Pampinelli:
My marriage is in name only. My wife was injured in a fire six years ago, and she lost most of her cognitive abilities. She has the mental capacity of a seven-year-old and will never recover.

Charlene Morris-Dempsey:
Oh. I am so sorry.

Peter Pampinelli:
I have come to terms with it, and have a lot of help for her. She is well taken care of and always will be. I will never leave her, but I still have needs to be met. And from what it sounds like on your end, so do you. So why don't we meet each other's needs, enjoying each other in the process?

Charley is stunned and speechless. She doesn't know which end is up. Never in her wildest dreams did she think when she started talking to Peter he was headed down this path. Charley's conscience is at war. On one hand, she rationalizes, her needs aren't being met at home. It's not like there is anything physical going on between her and Peter.

What's the harm in letting herself hear pretty words?

Her conscience isn't going to let her off the hook that easily. *Yes, you have needs that aren't being met, but you are married to another man whom you promised to love, honor, and cherish until death do you part. Do you remember that?*

Do you think Garrett would feel cherished if he thought you were flirting with another man? Her conscience continues. The warring part of her retorts, *Yes, yes, yes. I remember all of that. But he's not cherishing me, either. What's wrong with me getting a little satisfaction from someone else?*

With the war roaring in her head, she decides to respond to Peter with words that astound Charley herself.

Charlene Morris-Dempsey:
Hmmm ... sounds intriguing.

Peter Pampinelli:
You have no idea how intrigued I've been with you.

Charlene Morris-Dempsey:
I'm not sure I entirely understand what you are looking for from me. But, I could sure use a good guy friend who makes me feel as great as you do. Your sweet words put me on cloud nine. But right now, I need to go. I'm a little stunned, and I need to absorb what you have just said

Peter Pampinelli:
Just have fun with me. I so enjoy our chats and seeing your beautiful face peering at me from my computer screen.

Charley's heart is in her throat as she puts this thought down for Peter to read.

Charlene Morris-Dempsey:
I have a little confession to make ...

Peter Pampinelli:
Yes, little bellissima. What is your confession?

Charlene Morris-Dempsey:
Well, it's more of a question, really.

Peter Pampinelli:
Ask away.

Charley isn't sure she has the courage to ask the question, but since she has already started, there is no getting around it.

Charlene Morris-Dempsey:
Why do I get a silly, little schoolgirl thrill every time I see a message from you?

Peter Pampinelli:
Maybe it's because you look at my picture and wonder what it would feel like to have my lips on yours.

Charlene Morris-Dempsey:
Oh.

Peter Pampinelli:
Are you imagining that now?

Charley's face is on fire as the image of Peter kissing her comes into her head.

Charlene Morris-Dempsey:
I am. And my face is hot, and I'm blushing. I really do need to go. I need to absorb this conversation before I say anything I might regret.

Peter Pampinelli:
No regrets. Just have fun and enjoy. Ciao, Bella. I look forward to hearing from you soon.

Charlene Morris-Dempsey:
Bye.

The ball is in my court. She thinks to herself. *I will have to be the one to initiate contact the next time. Oh, what am I getting myself into?*

CHAPTER FOUR

LOGGING OUT OF FACEBOOK, Charley is completely confused by her recent conversations with Peter. Her head is spinning, and she feels out of balance. Charley shuts her computer down completely and gets ready for a run. She needs to go over the conversation that is squirreling through her brain. She throws her running clothes on, jams her feet into her running shoes, grabs her iPhone and bolts out the door, wanting and needing an escape from the reality on her computer.

Charley realizes she has no one she can turn to with this. She can't go to Gayle and get her opinion. Gayle would shut her down and tell her "I told you so" faster than she could say, "Bob's your uncle."

Is this the way to finding some happiness? Charley thinks to herself as her feet pound out a steady rhythm on the pavement.

It would be so easy to fall into a little harmless flirtation with him. He just makes her feel so good about herself. With Peter, there is no worry about doing or saying the wrong thing.

He's far away, and he only wants a little flirtation, her inner voice tries to convince her.

He's as lonely as you are, the voice continues, in a whisper. Only, for him, it has to be worse.

Charley wonders what really happened to his wife. She feels a strong pull of curiosity and decides to look into it when she gets home.

What kind of fire? What kind of cognitive abilities was he talking about? And wow … he's sticking by her. Does that make him a good guy for staying with her or a sleazeball for meeting his needs elsewhere? The thoughts come tumbling through her brain, one after another.

Charley pounds out five miles in record time. The swirling in her head makes her feet work even faster. She bounds in the door and up the stairs to the shower, washing away the sweat of her workout so she can get on with her day.

After showering, she dries her hair, dabs on a little makeup, and sits down at her laptop. She starts her search for fire victims in New York City with the last name of Pampinelli. Charley is at a loss, having no idea what Peter's wife's name is and no idea if the fire even happened in New York City.

She's feeling more like a stalker than anything else, but she has a raging curiosity about Peter's wife. Charley is not sure why she's so curious about the woman. She knows it's really none of her business, but she wants to know Peter's story. She knows her own saga. She knows why she feels compelled to get involved in an online romance. She guesses that's why she wants to know Peter's history.

Scrolling through the New York City news stories about fires is a daunting task—one she almost gives up until she sees a little article about Elsbeth Burke being injured in a fire at her summer residence in the Hamptons. Charley is not sure what attracted her to the story since the name isn't associated with Peter's at all. But she feels there is some driving reason for her to click on the link, and she believes she has found the answer in *The East Hampton Star*.

May 25, 2005
A fire broke out in a house on Little Plains Road nearly taking the life of the only inhabitant. Thirty-five-year-old Elsbeth Burke was rescued from a back bedroom of the residence as the fire raged around her.

Ms. Burke was found unresponsive and was transported via helicopter to Stony Brook Hospital's burns center. Her condition is unknown at this time.

The details are sketchy, but she is pretty sure this is Peter's wife. She begins to dig a little deeper using Elsbeth's name and finds a slew of stories about her and her family.

The Burkes own one of the most prestigious publishing houses in New York City, and they are on the front page of nearly every society section in the paper. Charley finds the engagement photo of Peter and Elsbeth. She is a stunning, willowy blonde. She has wide-set dark eyes and a short, straight bob.

She looks as if she lived in a world where pampering was the norm.

Charley can't imagine she was ever a gawky teenager. Elsbeth Burke seems like a very enviable woman. She has money, grace, looks, and a handsome husband. From the very beginning of their marriage, it seemed as if they were poised to rule all of New York City together.

There are so many photographs of them, going from gala to gala. The amount of money they donated to this cause or that cause was enough to make Charley's head spin. Charley and Garrett have a very nice life, live in a beautiful house, but the life Peter and his wife live is a world apart from Charley.

Charley continues looking through news articles and photos of the Burke-Pampinelli era. She stumbles across another story about the fire, dated two months after the first one.

July 26, 2005
The mansion that the Burke family used to call their summer residence was completely demolished. The fire department finally released the property back to the family after a two-month investigation into the blaze. The Burke family was eager to do something with the property so they could start to "heal and move forward," according to William Burke, head of the Burke Publishing Empire.

"The fire nearly took the life of our only daughter, and we just want to close this chapter and begin to live again." Asked how their daughter was doing, Mr. Burke responded, "She is doing as well as can be expected after suffering burns over sixty percent of her body. She nearly died from smoke inhalation in the fire. She will never recover cognitively. That is why we are so anxious to get rid of this house. All of the bad that has happened to Beth happened in that house. The house needs to be gone from our lives."

Investigators are at a loss as to what caused the fire. At this time, they have ruled the fire accidental, blaming faulty wiring on the massive blaze.

Questions still remain as to why Elsbeth Burke was at the house alone. Her husband, Peter Pampinelli, said they had planned to go out to celebrate Memorial Day weekend together and could not understand why she wouldn't have told him she was leaving a day early.

At this point, Elsbeth Burke is still recovering from her injuries, and it is not known when, or if, she will be released from the hospital.

* * *

Charley's workday is shot. She spent the morning talking to Peter and working out. Her mid-afternoon was spent reading stories about Peter and his wife. If she thought her mind was swirling before, it's nothing in comparison to where she is right now. She needs to get this out onto paper so she can be clearheaded when her kids and husband walk through the door.

Charley pulls out an old journal, one she hasn't used since well before she and Garrett were married. She doesn't want to mix this story up with her present-day life. This story needs to stay separate.

March 11
Crazy,

Charley begins ...
I think I am certifiably crazy. I should just shut him down.

Why don't I? Because I am reveling in the attention and admiration. He is making me feel so good about myself. I know I am walking around with some huge grin on my face. I can't remember the last time I felt this pretty, and I know it has nothing to do with anything I've changed. It has to do solely with the attention I'm getting. What does that say about me?

I think it says that I am far too dependent on what other people think of me. I think it means I should start therapy. I need to remember that I am more than how others view me.

Ah, crap. This isn't even helping today. I don't know why I'm letting this get to me. It's not like he suggested we run away together. All he suggested was a little harmless flirtation. I can do that. No problem.

With that, Charley closes that journal and puts it away.

As she is turning to leave her bookcase, she sees a journal she hasn't opened in quite some time, one she started right when she and Garrett first started dating. She pulls it out and begins to read what she wrote.

She is so engrossed in reading, she doesn't hear the door to their bedroom open. Garrett wanders in, saying hello as he pulls his scrubs off over his head, startling Charley in the process. Her journal flies out of her hands as she lets out an involuntary gasp.

"Sorry, Charley. I didn't mean to startle you. I thought you heard me come in," Garrett says.

"I was so focused on what I was reading I didn't hear a thing," Charley tells Garrett. "You're home early. I wasn't expecting you until dinnertime."

"The ER was empty, so I decided to come home and cook dinner. I enjoyed eating as a family last night, and I thought I'd try to arrange it again. I bought everything to make my famous mac and cheese. The kids love it. You love it. My thinking was to throw it together and see if I could entice everybody back to the table."

Charley tells him that sounds like a fabulous idea as she picks up her journal to put it away. Bookshelves fill her entire office area, which is airy and sunny with built-in window seats running continuously along the wall of the room. Under the window seats are bookcases. Bookcases also line the wall opposite the windows. She loves to be surrounded by books and her treasures. Her bookshelves are crowded but tidy. They are filled with old papers, journals, floor plans, photo albums—you name it, it is in her bookshelves. But she knows where everything is.

To Charley, organization is the key to keeping everything neat. Her journals are arranged chronologically, corresponding to the time period in her life running the circle of bookshelves around the room. Nobody really ever looks at them except for her, but if anything were ever to happen to her, the kids would be able to find her journals and follow her life along the path of her bookshelves. She gives her journal one last backward glance as she and Garrett make their way down to the kitchen to prepare dinner.

* * *

It has been a couple of days since she got her last instant message from Peter. Charley knew it would be up to her to initiate contact with him. She was trying to avoid the situation by not responding, but she knows that isn't going to work much longer. She is leaving in a week to go to New Orleans, and she needs to know how much to pay Peter for the ticket. Charley puts on her big-girl panties and logs into Facebook.

Peter is not logged in.

This makes things easier. *I'll just leave a message, and he can get back to me.*

Charlene Morris-Dempsey:
Hey stranger! Sorry I haven't been around much, but my mom duties have been keeping me busy. I'm trying to get everyone ready so I can go on this fabulous trip to New Orleans to hang out with some pretty cool people. ;-) Anyway, I remember you telling me at one time you had an extra ticket for me. I can't tell you how excited I am to go, but I also need to know how much I owe you for the ticket. Let me know so I can either send you a check or have enough cash to pay you back. Looking so forward to the game and hanging out with some good friends.

Charley hits send and get an immediate reply. *He must have just logged in.*

Peter Pampinelli:
Hey yourself! I was beginning to worry I had permanently scared you off, and you wouldn't be joining us. I'm glad to see I was wrong. As for the ticket, it's my treat. My publishing house is paying for them, so you can enjoy yourself without worrying about money.

Charley is stunned his message comes through so quickly. She didn't even see that he had logged in. Her response is just as quick.

Charlene Morris-Dempsey:
Wow! Peter, that is awfully generous of you. I don't know if I can accept, though.

Peter Pampinelli:
Ah, bellissima lady, let me do this for you. It would be my pleasure. I like treating my friends well.

Charlene Morris-Dempsey:
Hmmmm ... well, I'll need to think about it. If I do accept, I will need to figure out a way to pay you back in kind.

Peter Pampinelli:
Nothing would make me happier.

Charlene Morris-Dempsey:
Well, it just wouldn't do for you to be unhappy now, would it?

Peter Pampinelli:
No. It wouldn't. I would get my feelings hurt, and it just wouldn't be pretty.

Charlene Morris-Dempsey:
Well, then I accept your generous offer. Thank you VERY MUCH!

Peter Pampinelli:
It is truly my pleasure. Like I said, I enjoy treating my friends well. And I am beginning to consider you a very special type of friend.

Butterflies start floating around in Charley's belly at this point, and it's hard to catch her breath. She isn't exactly sure this is the right path, but it just feels so good.

Charlene Morris-Dempsey:
Why thank you, kind sir. And I'm beginning to think you're something a little special, too. I'm looking forward to seeing you in person in one week!

Peter Pampinelli:
I'm excited, too! I want to see your blue eyes sparkle when I tell you how pretty you are.

Knocked off balance for a minute but recovering quickly, Charley is able to respond.

Charlene Morris-Dempsey:
And I'm looking forward to hearing it!
I really like this whole flirting thing we have going on.

Peter Pampinelli:
I am too, my little bellissima friend. And I want to share some rules with you about it, if I may.

Charlene Morris-Dempsey*:*
Rules?

Alarms start ringing in Charley's head but she shuts them down. This is too much fun, and she's enjoying this too much to stop now.

Peter Pampinelli:
Yes, rules. Just a few, but I think I should share them with you. First, remember this is for fun. Have fun with me, and I will have fun with you.
Enjoy me, and let me enjoy you. There is no talk of love or a future. I will not fall in love with you, and I expect the same from you.
All of this fun sometimes leads to physicality. Be prepared.
Protect me, and I will protect you, always.
We are friends—always, even if we decide we no longer want to flirt.

Holy *shit!* Charley reads the instant message over and over again, not really believing what she is seeing. She has a hard time wrapping her head around this ... rules? *Really?* Who the hell does he think he is, Christian Grey?

Charley types her knee-jerk response without thinking ...

Charlene Morris-Dempsey:
Rules? Really?!? Are you kidding me?!? This is just supposed to be fun ... fun shouldn't have any rules. Have you turned into Christian Grey when I wasn't looking?

Peter Pampinelli:
No, little bella, I haven't turned into Christian Grey, but the thought amuses me. I put these rules out there to protect you ... to protect us.

Charlene Morris-Dempsey:
I see. I need to mull this over. I'm a little overwhelmed. When you said, "flirt" I thought you meant flirt ... and now, I need to get to work. Talk to you later! I just need to think a bit and collect my wits about me. OK?

And with that, Charley is gone. She doesn't stay around to see his response.

Peter Pampinelli:
OK, my dolce friend. Ciao, Bella!

* * *

Charley decides it's time to dig into her newest house with gusto. She needs to sink her teeth into something to take her mind off Peter. She'll deal with him when she returns home later and has time to collect her thoughts. Right now, though, it's time to get herself over to her client's house.

When she arrives, Charley realizes how exciting redecorating this house is going to be. She's never worked with this client before, and the finds they have stored in their attic make Charley's mouth water. The thought of unearthing these buried treasures and making their house something new and special brings a smile to her face. The layout of their house is perfect, open and airy with great flow, so she should have an easy time shifting furniture here and there.

Formulating her plan, Charley thinks about adding special touches and bringing new life back into the house they let get old and stale because of the kids. That is something Charley can never understand—letting the house go because of the kids. There are so many kid-friendly fabrics out there; it should never be a choice between kid-friendly and a beautiful home. She works all morning, feeling a great sense of accomplishment and is surprised when she checks her watch to see it's already one o'clock. She thanks her clients for letting her have so much of their time, packs her camera, her notes, and heads home.

As she steps into her house, Charley realizes she is famished and gets to work fixing herself some lunch. While eating, she lets her mind turn to figuring out how to handle this flirtation with Peter. In the midst of thinking about him and his rules, she remembers a journal entry she wrote years ago about rules between men and women. She has to admit she is more than a little stunned by the way this whole situation is playing out. Her head is telling her to run, but her ego is being stroked and cared for, so Charley loathes the thought of walking away from all of the attention. Her stomach is in knots as she walks upstairs to her office.

Charley looks at her bookshelves and remembers an entry she wrote years ago. Finding the journal is a snap, and Charley sits down to read through her entries. She laughs out loud at some of what she wrote so many years ago. Her "rules," she calls them.

How appropriate. Peter has his "rules." Hopefully, this will give me an idea for a rule rebuttal.

There's a lot of advice there, but not much she can use for her own guidelines regarding Peter, so she'll just have to wing it. She knows she needs to respond with edicts of her own. She's never been very good about quietly acquiescing to arbitrary rules, and these seem very arbitrary. Who needs written rules for friendships and flirting? Obviously, Peter does, so Charley closes her journals and begins to write her own set of guidelines.

Once they are done to her satisfaction, she logs into Facebook and makes sure Peter is offline. She doesn't want this to become a conversation. She wants it to be a monologue he can read later. Once she sees he's not online, she types in her own rules in a note to Peter.

Charlene Morris-Dempsey:
You set down your ground rules. I gave you a sketchy outline of what I expected, but you stunned me a little with your rules. Sooooo, here are mine.

I'm (usually) a very honest person. This is all new to me. But I'll be up front with you when things get overwhelming for me, which I'm sure they will.

Yes, flirt. Be fun with me. Have fun with me. I'll do the same with you.

Physicality is something I can't consider. Kisses lead to intimacy with me. Intimacy leads to feelings. Feelings lead to problems. I'm not interested in giving, or receiving, sloppy seconds.

So message away ... but they're my rules now, Skippy. If you want to come along for a flirty, fun little time, then jump on board. If my rules are too much, then you are free to go back to the way things were before. Friends always.

Once that is out of her system, she scrolls down the pages and notes her hometown friends' enthusiasm about the upcoming basketball tournament, and Charley can't help but feel a spark of excitement at the thought of her weekend ahead. As a thrill surges through her, she gets a text message from Garrett, and a pang of guilt pierces her, knowing her exhilaration is building because of Peter. Charley picks up her phone and reads Garrett's message.

2:23 p.m.
I'll be home this afternoon, but I'll have to come back to the hospital this evening. It's going to be a long day here.

Charley responds.

2:24 p.m.
OK, we're having pot roast, so you can have something to eat before you head back.

2:24 p.m.
Sounds great. Thanks! See you around 4.

Charley turns to her computer, logs out of Facebook, and gets back to work.

She works steadily until four o'clock when she hears the first of the footsteps in the door. Christina picked up the twins, Noelle, and Andrew from school today. Knowing Christina was going to be responsible for all of the kids, Charley let her take her Sequoia, and she kept Christina's little bug.

Charley greets all of her kiddos as they come into her office to tell her about their day.

She listens to each of them, marveling at their talkativeness. As they are all chatting with her, Garrett walks in the door of her office to say hello to his family. He tells Charley about the steady flow of patients coming in today and then excuses himself to get some dinner. With the kids' stories all told, they leave to start their homework. And Charley sits back, feeling a bit off-kilter by the whirlwind of activity that has just descended on her and left.

She needs a quick breather, so she decides to log into Facebook one last time before she tackles the chores of the evening. They have a full slate of activities, so Charley knows there won't be much time for relaxation between now and when the kids head to bed. As she logs in, she sees she has a message from Peter. Her heartbeat picks up speed as she opens it.

Peter Pampinelli:
Hey there. This is going to scare you, but I need you to call me. I have something I really need to talk to you about. My number is 523-732- 7462.

Peter Pampinelli:
Oh, you are gone.

With fear in her heart, Charley sees that he is still online, so she quickly sends him a message.

Charlene Morris-Dempsey:
I hate being scared! Everyone's home. Can I call you in a little while? It may be after I drop the twins at basketball? Around 6:15-6:30?

Peter Pampinelli:
Should be good. Thanks. This is just too much to text, and I really need to talk to you. It's about my wife. She is not well.

Charlene Morris-Dempsey:
Oh shit! I'll call as soon as I can.

Peter Pampinelli:
I just need a friend who will listen.

Charlene Morris-Dempsey:
I can do that. I'll talk to you soon.

With that, and still a little fear in her heart, Charley writes Peter's number down, then logs out of Facebook.

* * *

Charley races downstairs knowing her cheeks are probably flushed. They are blazing hot, and she is sweating profusely at the thought of talking to Peter. She can't imagine why he would need to talk to her about his wife, but she has to admit she is looking forward to hearing his voice even though the content of their chat scares her. Somehow, she manages to get the kids fed, sees Garrett out the door, and loads the twins into the car for basketball practice without anyone noticing her shaking hands and red cheeks.

With the twins safely ensconced in the confines of the basketball court, Charley nervously inputs Peter's number into her phone.

He answers on the first ring with a "So, how is Louisville, Kentucky?"

His voice is deep and rich and warm. The sound of it sends shivers down her spine as she imagines him speaking those sweet Italian words in her ear. She pulls herself quickly out of her reverie, focusing on Peter and his story.

Charley finds her voice hasn't deserted her completely, although it's much more breathy than she remembers it sounding.

"Yes," she responds. "I live in Louisville, Kentucky. I've lived here since I left for college. I took the path less traveled by and went to the University of Louisville. It just seemed to be a better fit for me. It's smaller, and the temperatures here are warmer."

Charley knows she is babbling, but she can't seem to stop the flow of words coming out of her mouth.

"So, tell me about your wife," Charley tries steer the topic back to Peter.

Peter's voice is low and slow. She can feel his pain through the phone. "My wife," he begins, "as you know, is not well. She had an incident this morning with her nurse, and I think I may have to move her to a nursing facility. I'm not sure we are fully capable of handling her anymore. She used to be fairly docile, but as time has progressed since her injury, she has become violent and dangerous. I'm just feeling a little guilty because I never thought I would have to make the decision to move her into a facility. I always thought we would be able to care for her here. But with her striking out against her nurse, I just don't see how that is going to be possible."

"Oh, Peter! I'm so sorry. How can I help you?" Charley wants to know.

"I just need to vent a little. I don't need any advice. I just need to talk this through." His voice sounds weary.

"I'm here to listen."

Peter goes on to tell Charley about their early times together, much of it she already knows, and she begins to feel even more like a snoop into his background. She was wrong about him. He is being very forthcoming about his life with Elsbeth. As she listens, she hears his voice become more and more listless. It must be so hard to care for someone so young who has no hope of recovery, especially when that person is your spouse.

After about twenty minutes of venting, Peter is all talked out about his wife, and he turns the conversation to Charley and their upcoming trip. His voice becomes more vigorous, and the tempo of his speech picks up.

"Charlene, I got your rules. You are one funny, but beautiful lady. If that is all you can handle, that's fine by me. I'm just happy you are willing to still keep me as your special type of friend. And I can't tell you how excited I am to see you next week. This trip is going to be one of the best I've ever taken. Have you been to New Orleans?" he asks.

"It's been a long time since I've been there. I went in college twice, once for spring break and once for Jazz Fest. I'm pretty sure I wasn't sober most of the time I was there, so from what little I remember, it's a wonderful city," Charley says with a laugh.

"What an engaging laugh you have, Charlene. It's very rich and throaty. I could listen to it all day."

Charley blushes and stammers as she says "Thank you. No one has really ever commented on my laugh before."

"Well, it matches your eyes—very alluring. It can really draw a guy in."

Charley's cheeks have now turned crimson as she tries to think of something witty to say. Not surprisingly, every witty remark escapes her.

Peter's next words send jolts of shock rippling through her body.

"With eyes that pretty and a laugh that sexy, I can only imagine how completely hot your panties must be," he says, with his rich, baritone voice caressing Charley's ear. Goose bumps undulate across her arms, and she has to shake her head to collect her thoughts.

There is no way Peter Pampinelli just said that to me. Before she knows it, those same words have escaped her mouth.

"Ah, Bella, I didn't mean to offend. It was very complimentary. You are a beautiful woman, and I like the thought of you looking gorgeous in your panties."

Charley finally finds her voice and manages to reply, "Peter, this is not the way I imagined this conversation going. We were talking about your wife, and now you say you are conjuring up images of me in my panties. How the hell did we get here?"

"Bella, Bella, Bella, I told you, I needed to vent. I did, and now I feel much better. But if this bothers you, we can change the topic. I don't want you to feel uncomfortable. I'm very used to my wife and my life, so I'm much better at compartmentalizing," Peter explains.

"I'm just a little shocked," Charley responds. "I have never been down this path before, so just bear with me as I try to find my equilibrium."

"All right, my sweet, I want to say 'delicious' friend, but I will refrain. I will give you time to get accustomed to my compliments, but I want you to know how sexy and gorgeous I think you are. And I can't wait to see you in person and tell you that again. So, you need to get used to it."

Charley's voice is feeble as she tries to answer. She finally squeaks out an "OK" as the twins come running up to her. Hearing the chaos building in the background, Peter tells her to go focus on her kids, saying to her he will talk to her later and signing off with his usual "Ciao, Bella." Hearing the words spoken rather than seeing them on paper sends a little thrill right to the pit of Charley's stomach. Her arms break out in goose bumps again as she signs off.

* * *

Oh, DEAR! Charley thinks for the thousandth time. *What the hell have I gotten myself into? I'm too ordinary for all of this. I'm just a mom. This is so far out of my realm, it's not even funny. I should just back out slowly and get on with my life.*

Her brain continues working a million miles a minute as the twins chatter happily in the backseat of the Sequoia. Every now and again, Charley throws in an "Uh-huh" or a "Hmm, that sounds interesting" just to keep them from truly breaking her concentration.

Charley decides she needs to figure out what do and how to move forward with this. How is she even thinking about venturing down this path? This is crazy!

What the hell are you thinking? Her conscience roars, as a wave of guilt rolls over her. She thinks about Garrett and their life together. *It's nice, but it's not this. It doesn't have the excitement and the butterflies anymore.* Charley is nearly invisible to Garrett, at least as someone he can think of as sexy, to him anyway.

To Garrett, I'm just the mom of his kids. But still, that little voice goes on to warn *It's a nice life you have with Garrett. The kids are fabulous, and you have a good, nice, honest life. What if Garrett finds out? What then? Your sweet life is gone! POOF! Buh-bye!* The little voice has ratcheted up its volume, now nearly screaming in Charley's head.

As she is thinking through everything, her phone's tone for a new text sounds. She glances at the screen and sees a message from a familiar number. She can't place whose number it is, but she knows she's seen it recently. Charley types in her passcode so she can see the message waiting for her. From Peter.

Oh, shit! He now has my number. Now I have two different ways for him to contact me that need to be monitored and worried about ... shit!

Gathering her wits, Charley focuses on her phone.

9:15 p.m.
My sweet, bellissima friend. Please don't worry about a thing. I will never talk about you, or our friendship to anyone. And I know you'll do the same for me. Please don't worry about all of this. And know that so many of your girlfriends probably have the same thing going. You have no idea how many women tell me about their "boy toys," as they call them. You are not the only woman who's experiencing a dry spell in your marriage. And sometimes it's OK to do something to spice up your life a little. This is going to be fun. Remember, I will protect you. And you protect me. Relax, and have fun with me. I so want to do the same with you.

"Well, shit, shit, shit, shit, shit!" Charley yells out in the confines of her bedroom. She doesn't know which way is up. She so doesn't want to give up all of the good feelings of Peter's flirting, but she knows, deep down inside, this is wrong. And what the hell does he mean, most of her girlfriends have "boy toys?" Is he kidding??

9:56 p.m.
What do you mean, most of my girlfriends have "boy toys"? I've never heard a thing about that!

9:58 p.m.
Of course, they're not going to say anything to you. They don't want you to think they have anything less than a perfect marriage.

9:59 p.m.
Then why would they talk to you about it? Why is it OK for you to know?

10:01 p.m.
Because I am a neutral, if not sympathetic, person, and they feel like they can talk to me.

10:04 p.m.
Interesting ...

10:06 p.m.
Besides, with some of these women, I have formed a very close bond. I spend a lot of time with them editing and working on their books, so they feel safe with me.

Charley is still not convinced that most of her girlfriends have "boy toys," so she decides she needs to talk to Gayle first thing tomorrow morning and pick her brain a little.

She responds to Peter one last time and hopes she comes off sounding worldly and self-assured, not scared and confused.

10:08 p.m.
All right, my sweet, although somewhat deluded friend, I need to go. I'm a little, OK a lot, out of my comfort zone, and I need to ponder all of this. I will talk to you soon.

10:10 p.m.
Ciao, Bella! We will talk more soon.

As the throbbing begins in her temples, Charley puts her head in her hands. She is beyond confused and behaving like a star-struck teenager.

CHAPTER FIVE

CHARLEY NEEDS TO TALK to Gayle. And her conversation doesn't need to focus on what's going on with her, but rather what Peter said. Do most women have "boy toys," or is that just Peter's way of making all of this seem OK?

As soon as the kids and Garrett are out the door for school and work, Charley picks up her phone and hits Gayle's number. She knows Gayle is probably on her elliptical trainer right now, so she'll have a captive audience.

"Hey there! How are you?" asks Charley, trying hard to sound nonchalant.

"I'm sweating to the oldies," replies Gayle with deadpan humor. Charley knows she's referring to the Richard Simmons exercise tape from years ago that they bought when they were roommates. They used it as a way to keep their minds off exercise while they were working out. It used to bring on fits of laughter as they watched Richard and his class "push and sweat!"

"Oh, just my thing. What oldies songs are you playing, to keep the sweat rolling?" Charley asks.

"A little lovin' here, and a little more lovin' there, just give me some lovin'," Gayle responds. Charley can hear her friend's labored breathing and the music cranked in the background.

Oh, how appropriate ... give me some lovin', indeed! For all of her bravado at calling her best friend, Charley is at a loss for words on how to begin this conversation. There's really no delicate way to start, so she decides to bite the bullet and dive right in. But before Charley has a chance to begin, Gayle asks her about the ticket to the basketball tournament.

Aww crap. With all of the craziness of the past twenty-four hours, she completely forgot she needed a cover story for Gayle.

Charley's response sounds a little lame, and she knows it. "Yes, I have a ticket, but Peter says his publishing house is paying for everyone. So, it's not a big deal."

What she said was partly true, Charley justifies to herself. Peter's company is covering the cost of the tickets, but she's just not sure if he's paying for everyone, or if it's just for "special" friends.

Gayle's voice brings her back to reality as she says, "Oh, Charley, I just think that's a bad, bad idea. You can't just let someone, especially a guy, pay for your ticket. It just doesn't look quite right."

"Oh, Gayle! You sound like an old fuddy-duddy. It's no big deal. He says he's paying for all of us, so it truly is not a big thing. And if he can afford it, why not let him?"

Charley's conscience smacks her upside the head and yells in her ear, *You have no idea if he's paying for everybody. You're just making shit up!*

Charley has to agree. She's making shit up.

"All right, Gayle. I'll ask again, and I'll find some way to make him let me pay him back." Which is no white lie. She really did tell Peter she would find some way to pay him back.

"OK, good. That makes me happy. I don't want you to feel obligated to Peter at all," Gayle responds.

If only she knew. It wouldn't be good. Gayle would be horrified to know the amount of contact she's had with Peter.

And again, Charley's conscience rears its ugly head and says *if a relationship has to be secret, you shouldn't be in it.* Part of Charley wants to smack the shit out of her conscience. *Why shouldn't I have just a little happiness? Why shouldn't I be able to accept compliments and flirt a little? I'm married, not dead,* she rationalizes.

Part of Charley wants to hang up now. Knowing what kind of a mood Gayle is in doesn't bode well for how this conversation is going to turn out, but it's too late. And Gayle would be suspicious if Charley said good-bye now. So, she just has to plug on and try to be as cool about her questioning as possible. But first, Charley needs to close out this topic by making sure Gayle is appeased.

"Oh, Gayle! I wouldn't feel obligated to him even if I did let him buy me a ticket. But I won't, so this conversation is moot. No worries, my friend!" As Charley finishes she hears the music switch to Uncle Kracker's song *Follow Me*.

How stinking appropriate. And before she knows it, Charley asks, "Hey, can you come over later? I'd love to have a glass of wine with you. I'll buy all the ingredients to make *rouladen* and *spaetzle* for all of us if you come help me assemble it. Then when we're done, you can take yours home with you."

"That is a fabulous idea, Charley. It's been a long time since we cooked dinner together. I'll come around four, and I'll bring the wine," offers Gayle.

"Wooo hooo! Two weeks in a row that I'm drinking wine in the middle of the week. I'm going to turn into an extra-large lush if I keep up this pace. I'd better get out there and pound out some miles if I'm doing wine and *rouladen*," Charley responds.

"Oh, Charley, you've got to stop being so hard on yourself. You have a fabulous figure. You eat well all the time, and I do mean *all the time*. You exercise to stay healthy. It's OK to splurge every now and again. It's not like you do this every day."

"What do you mean I've got to stop being so hard on myself?" Charley asks. "I just need to keep the middle-age spread from spreading too much, is all I'm saying."

Gayle counters with, "You, my sweet, are way too hard on yourself about food and drinks. You count every calorie. You save up calories for the weekend. I've seen you weigh your food and count out pretzel sticks to make sure you're only eating a serving size. I have to say, sometimes you drive me crazy in restaurants. I watch you eat exactly half of your meal, and the rest is either left behind or taken home. You never waiver from eating half, even if you've spent the entire day working out."

"Wow," Charley says, "where the heck did all of that come from? I didn't realize what I did was so noticeable to other people."

"Well, it is," Gayle continues. "I know you want to keep in shape and stay healthy, but I think you've taken things a step too far. So I'm *really* glad we're doing *rouladen* and wine tonight! And we'll talk more about this when I come over, but right now, I really have to jump in the shower and get moving. I'll see you at four, and I'm really looking forward to it."

"Yes, Gayle ... we will talk more about this later! I may just have to open up a can of whoop-ass on you when you get over here. You're making me sound like a crazy person!" Charley responds.

With laughter in her voice, Gayle says, "Well, if the shoe fits, my crazy friend! And with that, I have to go!! I'll see you soon! Bye!"

Charley hangs up with a feeble "Bye" and begins to mull over her conversation with Gayle and how she's going to bring up the whole "boy toy" issue that Peter implanted in her brain. She's really wondering how this whole afternoon is going to pan out now.

* * *

Charley wants to get some work done, exercise and shower before Gayle's arrival, but first she feels compelled to listen to Uncle Kracker croon through the lyrics of *Follow Me* after having just heard a snippet of it in the background while she was talking to Gayle. She grabs her iPod and scrolls through her playlist, knowing the song is somewhere in the depths of her music. She finally finds the song she so desperately wants to hear, cranks up the volume on the docking station, and sits back to absorb the words.

Charley shuts the song off halfway through, understanding now why she felt the need to hear it. The tune sticks with her all morning long, but one part plays over and over in her head, summing up how she's feeling. *He's not worried about the ring I wear because nobody knows, so nobody can care.*

"As long as no one knows," Charley muses out aloud.

* * *

Gayle shows up at four o'clock, and the *rouladen* making begins. It's an old family recipe that's been handed down for generations in Charley's family, and it's one that everyone loves, but preparation can be daunting if only one person is preparing the meal. With Gayle and Charley working side by side, it will be a piece of cake, and they each get to their tasks. They slice onions, pickles, and carrots, making neat little piles. They pound the thinly sliced beef even flatter, and then they smear each piece with Dijon mustard. Charley starts assembling the *rouladen* by putting a piece of carrot, a piece of pickle, a slice of onion, and a slice of bacon on each piece of beef. Gayle comes behind her and starts rolling and securing all of little meat pouches so the filling doesn't fall out while cooking.

The two old friends chat as they work, beginning with the topic of Charley's so-called "crazy" behavior when it comes to food.

"I can't believe you think I'm a little over the top about how I handle food," a defensive Charley says to Gayle as she is lifting her glass to her lips.

"Well Charley, you like to be a little too in control of your food. I've never seen you this obsessive about food. You used to eat to enjoy your meals, but now, you restrict so much of what you eat. I just about fell off of the elliptical trainer this morning when you said you wanted to make *rouladen*. You never eat carbs or bacon. And you *never* drink wine during the week. You seriously count every calorie that enters your body. At this point, it might not even be deliberate, but I watch you calculate every bite of food you take into your mouth when we're together. It has to drive Garrett insane. You've taken all the fun out of eating and now make it a boring chore—salads, low-calorie soups, fat-free this, lean that—no flavor at all."

Charley is a little taken aback but regains her composure enough to compose a retort. "I have to keep myself in shape. Garrett barely acknowledges me now. Just imagine if I got fat. He'd never look in my direction. Not that he really does now, but it would be even worse. He only likes those skinny model types. And I feel like I'm quickly becoming a middle-aged blob," Charley finishes with tears in her eyes.

"Oh, Charley, you are not becoming a middle-aged blob. You are a beautiful woman. And, in my eyes anyway, just a tad too skinny. You don't have that healthy glow anymore. You always look so pale. You could really stand to put on a few pounds, not lose a few pounds," Gayle says wrapping her friend in a hug.

Charley sheds a few more tears to help cleanse the negativity and sadness from her system before she playfully slaps Gayle on the rear, demanding they get back to work. As they finish putting together their fabulous meal, Gayle raises her wine glass to toast, "This will be the beginning of a beautiful friendship with meals for you."

While they are fixing dinner, the music takes them on a trip down memory lane. They have the 80s pop station playing on Pandora, and it's cranking out old hit after old hit after old hit. It's when Peter Gabriel's song *In Your Eyes* comes on that Charley tentatively brings up the subject of "boy toys" by way of asking Gayle if she believes most women they know are happy in their marriages. "I know that you are struggling with your marriage right now. It has to be ripping you apart inside. I think there are struggles in most marriages. The way each person decides to move forward determines whether a marriage will be happy or not. Each partner has to want to work toward happiness. You and Garrett will get there again. I see so much love between you and know you'll both work toward your happily ever after."

Charley's mind wanders back to the first time she heard Peter Gabriel sing *In Your Eyes*. She was sitting watching *Say Anything* on her VCR when John Cusack held the boom box up to his girlfriend's bedroom window, and Charley remembers thinking that was the most romantic thing she'd ever seen. She'd listen to the song over and over again just to experience the little thrill she got in her stomach every time she thought of someone standing outside her room playing that song for her.

As the song comes to an end, Charley lets a dreaminess wash over her, wanting to be completion in someone else's eyes. She wishes she had that kind of romantic hero for herself. "What if happy marriages are just a sham?" Charley wonders. "What if most people aren't really happy, but get their happiness somewhere else? Do you think that ever happens?"

"Are you talking affairs?" Gayle asks.

"No, no. Not affairs, just little bits of fun here and there. I've been hearing a lot about women who are taking on 'boy toys'—you know, just a little fun on the side," Charley finishes.

"A little 'fun on the side' is never a good idea, Charley," Gayle chides. "Only hurt can come out of that. Personally, I think it would be better to just divorce your husband and go from there, rather than fool around and risk your marriage."

"Well," Charley says, "What if you just used your 'fun' to enhance your own marriage? You know, spice things up a little."

"I don't think that's possible or fair. But I guess there is a segment of the population who finds satisfaction in that. Remember the *Oprah* episode from a couple of years ago about open marriages? Those couples seemed completely at ease about sleeping with other people. But that's not for me. And I would kill Jack if he ever cheated on me," Gayle declares, now a little worked up from the subject matter.

"And I'd be especially careful of anyone who told you that having a 'boy toy' is a good idea," Gayle finishes with a flourish.

Oh boy, Charley thinks to herself ... *maybe this isn't such a good idea.*

* * *

With the preparation of dinner complete and the bottle of wine finished, Gayle and Charley say their good-byes.

As Gayle is leaving, she offers some final advice, "Honey, I know things are stale and kinda sucky in your marriage right now, but please don't do anything you'll regret. I know you think Peter is gorgeous, and he is, but be careful with him when you go to New Orleans. I don't want to see you hurt anyone, and I certainly don't want to see you get hurt. You are a married woman, and married women don't take on 'boy toys.' Things will get better with Garrett, I promise. Garrett's a good guy. He's just kind of lost his way in this marital world. When you get back, we'll sit down together and figure out how to get your marriage back on track. Until then, I'm begging you to be careful."

Charley hugs her friend tightly as she says good-bye and watches her walk out the door.

* * *

Charley's phone lights up with a message from Peter.

10:19 a.m.
Salut, bellissima! How are you this morning?

With excitement building, Charley quickly responds.

10:20 a.m.
I am very well this morning! How are YOU?

10:22 a.m.
Ah, my deliziosa little friend, I am so excited to see you tomorrow. When does your flight get in?

Charley is more than ready to go, and if she could leave right now and head to New Orleans to see Peter, she would. Her response doesn't mask her enthusiasm.

10:23 a.m.
I am SOOOO excited to see you, too!! It's going to be an awesome weekend, and I can't wait. I wish we could all leave right now. But we can't, so all I can tell you is my flight gets in at 5:42 p.m. tomorrow afternoon.

10:26 a.m.
PERFECT! My flight gets in at 5:00 p.m., so I'll get my rental car and wait for you. And then we can ride to the hotel together.

Holy shit, I'm going to see him as soon as I step off the plane. He's going to be waiting for me. Oh my God! This is really it. The day is almost here. Her mind is doing backflips, while her heartbeat accelerates, but she responds as coolly as she can.

10:28 a.m.
That sounds FABULOUS! I can't wait!

10:30 a.m.
Make sure to wear a skirt, so that if it blows up, I can see your sexy panties.

Charley's face floods with color as she tries to think of a witty comeback. She types and hits send before her bravery escapes her.

10:31 a.m.
I'll make sure to wear my pink lace boy shorts ... those should be sexy enough for you. ;-)

She can't believe what she has just sent. This is so out of character for her. What is getting into her? Is she really going to go down this "boy toy" path?

Oh, yes ... that little voice in her head says to her, *Yes, you are going to head down this path. It'll be so much fun.* And with that thought flitting through her brain, the war in her head begins. *No, I'm just going to play with fire. It's fine. I can handle a little flirting and dabbling in fun.*

10:33 a.m.
I can't wait to see them for myself! All right, Bella ... I need to get going. I need to pack. I can't wait to see you tomorrow. A little more than 24 hours, and I will get you all to myself!

As she responds, Charley's insides flutter at the thought of being alone in a car with Peter. Knowing she will have him all to herself for a little while makes her pulse quicken.

10:35 a.m.
OK, Peter! I'll see you tomorrow! Looking forward to it.

* * *

God, he can't wait to bury himself inside of her. She's just so ripe for the picking—so naïve and trusting. She's never been down this path before, and it's up to him to make sure her experience is beyond anything she's ever known. She'll need to be persuaded a bit and may need a little medicinal courage, but it will be well worth it in the end. His need to have her in his collection grows more and more every time he talks to her. The others in his collection are more jaded and cynical. He'll have to be careful with this one, though. Her naïveté is charming, but it could also be problematic. He needs to make sure she understands there is no talk of love in all of this. Becoming part of his collection is purely for physical pleasure. He wants her to experience that pleasure with him. He wants to hear her moans beneath him as he brings her to the brink of orgasm and back. He is rock-hard at the thought of her legs wrapped securely around his waist as he thrusts himself inside of her until she cries out with her release.

He needs to turn his attention elsewhere for now. He wants his sexual needs unmet for today. He wants to know he is raw and ready for her this weekend. He'll have her soon. Very soon.

* * *

The realization hits Charley as she is packing—the time to leave is *so* close. She needs to finish organizing and making sure she has just what she needs. She has ordered a new University of Michigan jacket so she has something to wear to the game. She also bought herself some brand-new Lucky jeans. They seem to emphasize every curve on her backside and make her feel about two hundred shades of sexy, especially knowing she'll have a pair of pink lace boy shorts underneath them. She's still deciding what to wear on the plane. It's chilly in Louisville, but she'll be traveling into warmer temperatures. She can't get over Peter's request to "wear a skirt, so if it blows up, I can see your sexy panties" off her mind. Charley's suitcase becomes fuller and fuller, as she throws more and more clothing in, making sure she has just what she needs to survive the weekend.

With her bag packed, Charley has finally decided on her outfit for the plane. She has a knee-length denim skirt that buttons up the front. She'll wear that with her cowboy boots and a light pink cashmere sweater with a lace cami underneath. Charley zips up her suitcase, puts her makeup kit in its case, and heads downstairs to make sure every t is crossed and every i is dotted in her schedule. The last thing she needs is a snafu in her organizing.

Her schedule looks perfectly organized and ready for inspection. Charley heads to the kitchen to make sure the dinners she has prepared are in the freezer.

Oh sweet Jesus, Garrett, Charley thinks to herself. He's been around so infrequently this past week that she has pushed thoughts of him, and any feelings of guilt, to the far recesses of her mind. Charley stops mid-stride when she realizes her excitement about the weekend is all because of Peter. She can't wait to see him, spend time with him, hear his sweet words for her and maybe ...

"NO," Charley says out loud, stomping her foot, "I won't think about that. I'm just going to New Orleans to have fun, watch some basketball and just ... oh, who the hell am I kidding? I'm going because I get to see Peter," she finishes, quietly and lamely.

Feeling a bit ashamed of herself, Charley redoubles her efforts to make sure the house is just as Garrett likes it—neat and tidy, smelling heavenly and completely organized.

Charley sets to making her famous chicken potpie, a true family favorite that has won her accolades from everyone who has tasted it. Once she has the chicken gravy made, she takes the cooked chicken out of the fridge, pours it into the lasagna pan with the vegetables, and tops it with her homemade biscuit topping. She pops it in the oven and turns to make a batch of chocolate chip cookies. Even though she won't touch a bite of any of this, the cooking and baking eases her conscience a little as her excitement grows.

CHAPTER SIX

THE DAY DAWNS bright and blustery. Charley rolls out of bed and begins her work to get the family out of the house. While she is fixing breakfast and lunches for the kids, Garrett comes in holding Charley's list of instructions for the weekend. When she see the expression on his face, she realizes there is trouble brewing.

As Garrett's words bite out at her, she tenses up. "Jesus Christ, Charley, I thought you told me this weekend was going to be easy for me. It seems like there are more tasks on here now than when you are home. I have to drive the twins to the dentist tomorrow? Seriously? That is something you should have rescheduled. And then on Saturday, I'm taking Noelle and her friends to the mall? Charley, this list is crazy. I only picked two of the inane tasks you have on here. This list goes on and on. You need to pare it down. I'm not doing all of this shit."

Charley tries to keep her voice calm, knowing that if she blows up, this will become a much bigger deal than it needs to be.

"Garrett, it's OK. Really. All you have to do is drop Noelle and her friends off at the mall. Christina is picking them up, but she can't drive them because she has to go to a study session for the SATs in the morning. She'll be done by the time the girls are ready to leave the mall. It's not that big of a deal.

Christina will have the Sequoia, so she can fit everybody in. A lot of what is written down is for your information, and nothing you need to take care of. I just wanted to let you know what the schedule is like and who is taking care of what for me. I called in a lot of favors to get the kids' schedules taken care of for you. As for the twins' appointments, I needed to keep them for tomorrow. It would have taken two months to reschedule their dental exams. Chandler is complaining of a toothache, so I didn't want to push things back. I'll call your mom this morning and see if she can take them, if that would make things easier for you."

"When is Gayle coming to get the boys?" Garrett wants to know.

"It's all written down on the schedule, but I'll give you the condensed version right now," Charley explains.

"Gayle will get the boys from school this afternoon, take them home with her, have them spend the night, and send them off to school tomorrow. The twins' dental appointments aren't until eleven, so if your mom can take them, I'll see if Gayle can pick them up at school and meet her at the dentist's office. After school, Gayle will get the boys from the bus stop, and she will have them until I get home from the airport. I'll pick them up on my way home. Is all of this sounding a little easier? I truly tried to make it as simple for you as I could, but there are some things I just couldn't rearrange."

"It's fine, Charley," Garrett replies, still with a bite to his words. "I just wasn't expecting such a long list."

Charley watches Garrett get ready to leave for work. She knows he's still in a huff. She can feel it in the loud slam when he walks out the front door. *His weekend is shot to shit because of me. He thinks he has so much work to do, but I've taken care of the majority of the arrangements. There's really not that much more he'd be doing if I were home. God, he seems to be forgetting he helped me plan this trip, but now that's it's here, it seems like he wants my weekend to be miserable.*

Charley feels like the morning interrogation will never end and is relieved when Garrett's car pulls out of the driveway. The more she thinks about how Garrett treated her, the angrier Charley becomes. She doesn't go away often, or ever, and here Garrett is piling a load of crap on her shoulders right before she's due to leave. Her mood is sour, and her feelings toward Garrett border on really pissed off and extremely pissed off. Somewhere in the far reaches of her brain, a tiny voice can be heard telling Charley in a soothing voice that Peter is not far away.

Charley puts the kitchen back in order and heads up to shower. She gives her legs, her armpits, and her private parts a good, thorough shave, shaking off the razor when she is done so she can pack it in her makeup bag. After making sure her hair is shampooed and well conditioned, Charley steps out of the shower, wrapping herself in a big fluffy towel. She dries off her body and her hair, applying her favorite moisturizer as she goes. Charley sprays a leave-in conditioner into her hair, blowing it dry into a mass of soft waves. Next, she artfully applies her makeup and perfume. She packs those things away in her suitcase when she is done. Dressing carefully, Charley makes sure her outfit is exactly what she envisioned. She is satisfied with her reflection in the mirror, except for her pale face, which no amount of blush can cover. Her heart is still a little dull from the emotionally draining morning she had with Garrett, as she carries her suitcase down the stairs.

But before she can leave, she needs to put in the obligatory phone call to her mother-in-law. Charley's blood pressure starts to rise as she hits the number on her phone, connecting her to Garrett's mother. Her annoyance at Garrett grows with each ring of the phone. Finally, Pam picks up, and Charley manages to find her sweetest voice, hoping Pam finds it sincere.

"Hey, Pam! It's me! How are you?"

Charley sits and listens as Pam rambles off one list of complaints and rolls into another. Charley interjects the appropriate sympathetic noises, as the stories about Pam's declining health, deteriorating memory, and lack of people to help her out continue.

"It's almost sinful," Pam laments. "Here I am surrounded by family, but there is never anyone around," she finishes spitefully.

Well, maybe if you weren't such an evil witch, I would be more inclined to encourage my kids to come around to help you out. Charley would never dare voice that opinion out loud, but she thinks it every time she has to interact with her mother-in-law.

Mindful of her need to be at the airport soon, Charley is finally able to interject long enough to get her Pam's attention.

"Oh my gosh, Pam. It sounds like you are having a rough time right now. I'm so sorry Garrett hasn't called or visited lately. I had no idea you hadn't spoken to him in over two weeks. I'll make sure he gives you a call to check on you. And if you want, I can send Christina over this weekend. Maybe she can help you go through some things in your house so it feels a little more organized, and then you'll know where everything is." Charley knows she will pay dearly for the promises she is making, but she needs to appease Pam so she can make Garrett happy. Charley dreads the thought of coming home to a pissed-off Garrett.

"I know you have a lot on your plate right now, but I'm headed out of town for the weekend to a conference." Charley slips a little white lie in there, knowing it will be easier to get Pam's help if she thinks this trip is work related. She reminds herself to let Garrett and Christina know so they don't blow her cover.

"And I was wondering if you could meet Gayle at the dentist's office with the twins. Gayle will pick them up from school and bring them to the dentist, but Garrett would like for you to be there while the kids are examined." Another white lie.

Charley hopes she doesn't burn in hell for the fibs she's telling her mother-in-law and reminds herself there are far worse reasons for her to burn in hell, and one of them is named Peter.

Charley knows the odds aren't really in her favor in asking Pam to take care of the twins, but she's willing to take the risk so she doesn't have to think about coming home to a pissy Garrett. Pam has never really liked the twins, which is totally baffling to Charley since they both look like spitting images of Garrett. She braces herself, waiting for Pam's answer.

Charley is more than relieved when she hears the exhalation of air followed by a gruff, "Yes, I'll take care of the twins, but I expect to be able to see the other grandkids this weekend too, especially Christina. I look forward to seeing her at my house on Saturday afternoon," Pam finishes.

Thankful to have that taken care of, Charley signs off with Pam and sends out three texts. The first one goes to Garrett.

11:10 a.m.

Talked to your mom. She will take care of the twins' dentist appointment tomorrow. I told her I was going to a work conference. Play along for me, if you would. And call her, please? I didn't know you hadn't talked to her in weeks. I'm the one who gets yelled at when you don't call. So CALL HER!

The second text goes to Gayle.

11:13 a.m.
Hey! I know you said you'd keep your days open while I'm gone, just in case my kids need you. Well, guess what? They'll need you. The twins have a dentist appointment that I thought Garrett could take care of, but he can't. I don't want to reschedule, so can you take them to Dr. Yang's office, please? Pam will meet you there.

As Charley is typing her third text to Christina, she gets a response from Gayle.

11:15 a.m.
You mean to tell me your mother-in-law is going to help YOU out?? I'm shocked!

11:16 a.m.
She's only doing it so she has something to hold over us. And because I promised Christina would go by and help her out over the weekend. I'm texting her right now to tell her the news. I don't think she'll be happy, but there's nothing I can do.

11:18 a.m.
So why, exactly, can't Garrett take care of the twins?

11:19 a.m.
He says the list is too much work for him. He was snippy about my whole schedule, so I just figured it was easier to get you to cover it than to worry about him being irritated with the kids and me. Thanks for helping me out!

11:20 a.m.
My pleasure, my friend! But I think when you get back, you and Garrett need to have a serious talk about your marriage. He's acting like a shit.

11:21 a.m.
Yes, he is, and I think you're right—we will need to discuss our future when I get back. But right now, I need to run so I can catch a plane! THANKS again for helping me out! You're the BEST! See you when I get home!

11:22 a.m.
Have fun, and don't do anything I wouldn't do.

Charley's heart nearly stops as she reads those words. Gayle wouldn't do *any* of what Charley is doing, but Gayle also wouldn't put up with her husband being such a shit to her. She would have kicked Jack's ass a long time ago if he treated her so poorly. Charley shakes her head and gets back to the task at hand—one last text to Christina.

11:28 a.m.
Hey, sweetie. I know you won't get this until after school, but I wanted to tell you that I talked to Grandma today, and she really misses you. She asked me if you would go by her house over the weekend to help her organize a little since you're so good at it. I'd really appreciate it if you would visit her on Saturday after you get back from the mall. If Noelle goes with you, it shouldn't be too bad. Trust me, I'll make it worth your while.

Charley knows that line will have price tags from Christina's favorite stores all over it, but she's at a loss. She needs to get moving. There's a plane to catch, and it's not going to wait around for her.

Grabbing her winter-white coat, Charley throws it on, heading out the door without looking back.

She throws her suitcase into the trunk of Christina's little bug, pulls out of the driveway, heading to Louisville International Airport. She arrives earlier than expected. Traffic had been non-existent on the highway, which allowed her to make great time. Charley pulls into a spot, as the song *Bruises* by Train and Ashley Monroe comes on the radio. The opening words strike her heart—old high school friends seeing each other for the first time in a long while. He still thinks she's beautiful. Just like Peter tells her. *Is it a sign?*

Charley stays put listening to the song until she gets to the line "leaving you makes me wanna cry."

Will she want to cry when she leaves Peter? She grabs her suitcase and heads to the terminal to check in.

Once she is through security, Charley heads to the airport bar for a nerve-calming drink. She knows it's early for alcohol, but she really doesn't care. Part of her is still in a funk about the good-bye with Garrett, but the other side of her is beyond nervous about seeing Peter in less than five hours. The bartender sets a Jamison and diet ginger ale in front of her, and she takes one long swallow, hoping this is the ticket to regaining her excitement.

Charley's flight is called on time. Boarding the plane, she sits down to finally contemplate what she really wants to get from Peter out of this upcoming weekend. She needs to be careful, she knows, remembering Uncle Kracker's words "As long as no one knows, then nobody can care." Charley wonders to herself, *Is it true that as long as it's a secret, then nobody will care?* The words of her conscience roar in her head. *Of course that's not true, you dumbass! If it were true, everyone would be having affairs. Do you remember nothing I tell you? If a relationship has to be secret, you shouldn't be in it!* Her conscience finishes loudly, her words reverberating through her brain.

* * *

As the cabin door closes, Charley's phone dings with a text from Peter.

2:15 p.m.
Hello, Bella! I will see you in less than four hours. I can't wait! Send me a picture of what you're wearing, so I can find you easily.

How the hell am I supposed to send him a picture of what I'm wearing?

She is trying desperately to think of a way to photograph herself, when all of a sudden, it hits her. She can hold her camera up over her head, take the photo aiming down at her body, leaving her head out so she doesn't have to worry about looking nervous or goofy in the picture.

2:16 p.m.
Just so you know, I felt incredibly foolish taking that picture on a plane in front of everyone, but here it is. This is what I'm wearing today.

2:17 p.m.
You wore a skirt. I like that. And your legs are gorgeous. They look so smooth. I can't wait to really feel them.

Holy, holy, holy SHIT, Charley thinks to herself looking at the picture she just sent. The slit on the front of her skirt looks incredibly high, and the cleavage under the cashmere sweater looks like it's pushing up, threatening to spill out of her bra. Maybe it's just in her mind, but a sinking feeling starts churning in the pit of her stomach. Peter's next words confirm what she suspects.

2:18 p.m.
Wow, bellissima, your sweater is breathtaking. I love how it seems to caress you in all the right ways.

"Aw, I screwed that one up, didn't I?" Charley mumbles to herself as a young man sits down next her and glances at her bare legs. Charley tugs on the fabric of her skirt as her phone dings again.

2:19 p.m.
I knew I was looking forward to seeing you, but now I'm REALLY looking forward to seeing you! Ciao, Bella. See you soon. I'll take good care of this picture, I promise.

2:20 p.m.
You can just delete that picture, you know? It wouldn't hurt my feelings at all.

2:21 p.m.
Ah, Bella, why would I do that? Your picture will keep me company until I get to see you.

Shit, damn, fuck! Shit, damn, fuck! The words go rolling through Charley's mind like the credits in a movie. These are the words she relies on when she gets really wound up and irritated. This is one of those times. Charley is beyond wound up and wishing the flight would get underway so she could order another drink. She doesn't know why she's so upset about a picture, but she is. It captured everything in just the wrong way. She wasn't really spilling out of her top, and her legs are really not *that* bare. But that damn picture makes her look like she's nearly undressed. And now she's really nervous.

Once the flight is airborne and beverage service begins, Charley orders a rum and Diet Coke. Sipping it slowly, she begins to wonder what is really going to happen when she sees Peter. Charley's face flushes as she fantasizes about him kissing her. She wonders what his hands will feel like as he wraps her in a sweet hug. Goose bumps rise up on her arms as she imagines his breath in her ear saying "Ah, Bella. I'm so glad you're here."

Her excitement is palpable as the irritation from earlier recedes with each sip of her drink. Charley's muscles relax as she imagines over and over again how this scene in the airport will play out.

In an attempt to settle down, Charley pulls out her laptop and begins to work on her newest house. But she can't focus. She becomes fidgety, constantly tugging her skirt down and pulling up on her sweater.

God, I'm so nervous. I'm going to have to slather on another layer of deodorant before I meet up with Peter.

Her armpits are sticky, and her stomach is doing flip-flops, making her feel like she's about ready to vomit. Realizing that trying to get any work done is futile, Charley puts her computer away and closes her eyes. All she can picture are Peter's lips moving toward her as he leans in to envelope her in a hug as she steps off the airplane.

Her eyes fly open. She excuses herself past her seatmate and heads to the restroom with her makeup bag tucked into her purse.

Charley takes a long hard look at herself in the mirror as she stands in the airplane's lavatory. Her hair is falling in loose waves around her shoulders. The soft pink of the sweater lends itself well to her overall appearance, highlighting the heightened color in her cheeks and balancing the dark blue of her eyes.

Charley pulls out her makeup bag to do a few touch-ups here and there, making sure to reapply deodorant and touch behind her ears with her Tuca Tuca perfume. Satisfied that she looks and smells exactly as she wants, she makes her way back to her seat to finish her rum and Coke and wait for the plane to land.

The flight attendants make their final call for trash and let the passengers know the flight is descending into New Orleans. Charley touches her cheeks, knowing they are flaming hot and hoping to cool them a little with her ice-cold hands. She puts her things away, stows her bag underneath her seat, and sits back waiting for the plane's wheels to hit the tarmac. To Charley, it seems to take forever to taxi to the jetway.

As the plane makes its way to the terminal, Charley reaches in her purse and pulls out her phone. Her fingers nervously drum across the surface of the glass. Her heart pounds in rhythm with the spinning icon while she waits for her phone to come back to life. The time it takes for the captain to turn off the fasten seat belt sign drags out even longer than it took for them to taxi in. Charley's phone dings open, and passengers start streaming out into the airport.

Standing on wobbly legs, Charley is thankful for the few-minute reprieve she will have before seeing Peter, and she makes her way into the airport bathroom to tuck stray hairs back in place and have one last look at herself before she makes her way out of her own world and toward the point of no return.

CHAPTER SEVEN

CHARLEY WALKS SLOWLY toward baggage claim. Peter knows her flight is here. It's posted on all of the screens, so she sees no need to text him. When she finally gets in sight of baggage claim, she can see him clearly across the way. He is sitting down texting, so she has ample opportunity to observe him. He is far more handsome than she remembers—the gray at his temples lend him a distinguished air. His dark hair falls softly across his forehead. His long fingers move gracefully across the phone as he types quickly and effortlessly. With his concentration broken, he looks up to see Charley headed for him. He stands with a smile on his face, walking toward her, and all of Charley's visions soon come to fruition.

Peter quickly closes the gap between them with a determined step. Wrapping his arms around her waist, he pulls her toward him. He is much taller than Charley remembers. She has to stand on her tiptoes to absorb the full effect of his embrace. Feeling him inhale her perfume she hears him say, "Ah, mia bella signora, you smell divine." Charley's heart races as those words caress her ear. She pulls back slightly to thank him when his mouth descends on hers. It is a sweet, gentle kiss but with an air of propriety. Charley is in a daze as she pulls away fully, having thought about being kissed by him, but not truly expecting a kiss as a greeting. Lifting a lock of hair away from her face, Peter exclaims, "You look absolutely beautiful, Charlene." Her full name on his lips sends a shiver down her spine as his hand strokes her cheek and travels lightly down her neck to the curve of her breast resting under her sweater. His finger traces lightly across the top of her camisole as he says, "Your picture earlier didn't do you justice."

Charley is struck dumb, rooted in her spot. Her feet are firmly planted, and she doesn't think she could move them if she tried. She has no idea how to respond. Things are moving quickly away from her grasp of reality.

Finally, she clears her head enough to find her voice. "Oh my. That wasn't exactly how I had that planned out, but I'm glad I had a breath mint."

Peter laughs a low deep chuckle and grabs her hand, pulling her toward the carousel where her luggage is expected.

Charley can feel her face flush with a rush of color. Her breath quickens as she takes in the darkening of Peter's eyes. Her voice is low and breathy as she says, "What kind of thoughts are going through your head?"

"You'll just have to wait and see, now won't you?"

She feels his eyes rake over her. A small thrill shoots through her, and she feels exhilarated at the thought of being the object of his desire.

"I hope your flight was easy and you weren't stuck sitting next to some troll from under a bridge. I'm sure you must be hungry, though," he says.

Charley is thrown a bit off-kilter by the ease with which he seems to change gears but easily gathers her thoughts. *God, yes I'm hungry—but not for food. I could go on all day hearing his voice in my ear and feeling his strong muscular body pressed up against mine.*

Instead she answers with a "Yes, Peter. I'm starving! The food on the plane was non-existent." *If I don't get something to eat soon, this day is not going to end well after those two drinks I had earlier.*

Peter grabs Charley's bag for her and leads her to his rental car. They walk through the airport parking garage hand in hand. As they're walking, Charley notices for the first time how tall Peter really is and how big his hands are. Her heart starts beating faster as she lets the softness of his fingers caress her palm. They stop beside a Jaguar XFR. Charley has no idea what any of those letters mean, but she does know it's a drop-dead, stunning car in sparkling silver. Charley's jaw just about hits the floor when Peter pops the trunk with the key fob. He releases Charley's hand, grabs her bag, and puts it in the trunk. When he is finished putting her bag away, he takes Charley's elbow and walks her to the passenger side of the car and opens the door. She's not used to the social graces men can display toward women, and she feels more than a little pampered. Peter walks around to the driver's side, slides effortlessly into the car, starts the engine, and pulls out of the parking garage.

As they're leaving the parking lot, Peter turns to Charley and says, "I know this great little place. It's called Parasol's. Do you like New Orleans-type food? Po' boys and muffaletta sandwiches?"

"Oh my gosh!" Charley responds. "I love a muffaletta! We have this great little place back home, and they make a mean sandwich."

"Good, then it's settled. We'll go there and grab a bite before we head back to the hotel," Peter says as he pulls over.

Charley suggests, "I can program the GPS for you, if that's why you're pulling over."

"No, that's OK. The first thing I need to do is this." Peter reaches across the seat and pulls Charley to him, covering her mouth in a searing kiss. It has been years since she has experienced a kiss quite like this.

Hungry. Raw. Demanding. Charley breathes in his cologne, as her senses are about to explode. His tongue caresses the deep recesses of her mouth, sucking, swirling, tasting, and teasing. She pulls back a little and opens her eyes to find Peter's dark brown ones locked on hers. They seem to burn with passion and desire, turning them nearly black. Charley's heartbeat is frantic when she realizes she has just kissed another man.

Peter must have read the conflicting emotions in Charley's eyes because he pulls away and lets her slide back to her seat, apologizing as she moves over, "I'm sorry, Charlene. I didn't mean to come on so strong, but the scent of your perfume kept pulling me closer and closer. I needed to inhale your sweet fragrance, and it just led to that kiss. And what a kiss that was. Your perfume is intoxicating. I couldn't control myself with you smelling so *dulce*. It's not fair for you to smell so good. What's the name of your perfume?"

Charley is lost in a sea of emotions. Guilt and shame are coursing through her, as are lust and longing. Although her world has just been turned upside down, she still has the wherewithal to answer his question. "My perfume is called Tuca Tuca."

Peter's laugh rings through the car as he says, "You're kidding, right?" His voice becomes quiet and gentle. Charley feels it's almost as if he knows he needs to calm her nerves.

Charley's voice is low and breathy as she answers Peter's question, "No—that is really the name. Why does that surprise you so much?"

"*Tuca Tuca* is a catchy, little Italian song that my father used to sing to my mother. I don't remember the entire song, but I do remember some romantic moments in our house when my father would perform it." A knowing smile plays across Peter's lips. He begins to hum the tune, reaching across the confines of the car and caressing Charley's cheek as he sings to the tune, "I want you. And when I look at you, you know I know what I want from you," Peter lowers his hand and continues with his eyes smoldering with desire, "Of course the song is in Italian, but that's the gist of what it's all about. It has a dance that goes along with it, allowing dancers to get to know each other better. Did you know that about your perfume when you bought it?" he asks.

Charley chokes on his words. "I want you" and "allowing dancers to get to know each other better" play through her head.

Oh, shit, Peter must think I did that on purpose! She stumbles and stammers, trying to explain that it was a gift from her kids at Christmas. They know how much she likes violets, and this perfume was right up her alley, filled with the fragrance of ripe violets.

"Ah, sweet Bella. I will have to show you a video of the dance later, and maybe we can learn it together," Peter suggests, his eyes smoldering.

A little thrill runs through Charley, followed by a pang of guilt. She's in way over her head, and now she knows just how much. She needs to proceed with caution, but the feeling of being so desired is intoxicating.

Peter breaks Charley's spell, "All right, bella signora. Let's go eat. You're famished, and so am I."

With that, he types in the address to Parasol's, and they leave the airport behind them.

* * *

Peter keeps the conversation light as they race through the streets of New Orleans. With a name like Parasol's, Charley is half expecting a restaurant similar to Butterfly Garden Cafe at home—quirky and eclectic. She is not expecting a white clapboard building with green shutters. Once inside, Peter leads her inside by the hand, and they're seated immediately. Her stomach rumbles so loudly she is sure Peter probably hears but is too polite to say anything. The waitress appears out of nowhere to take their drink orders. She turns first to Peter, who orders a Guinness, and then she turns her attention to Charley, whose thoughts drift back to her Jamison and diet ginger ale at the airport earlier that day. Charley decides that will be her drink of choice in this Irish pub in the middle of New Orleans.

Charley and Peter sit together comfortably, bringing each other up to date on the last twenty-four years of their lives. Even though Charley has seen him at high school reunions, their paths never intersected. Charley always stayed safely within the confines of her group of high school girlfriends. She would see Peter across the room, always aware of his incredible good looks, but she never really tried to get to know him better.

Peter fills Charley in on more of his wife's struggles over the past six years, going into further detail about the fire and her injuries. He's brutally honest about his wife, Beth's, prognosis and their marriage. It is in name only, he repeats. Beth is the only child of a very wealthy publisher in New York City. Her father had been grooming her to eventually take over the day-to-day operations of their empire when the fire struck, nearly killing her. Peter was working side by side with her so they could learn the inner operations of the publishing house, and he knew he couldn't leave Beth or her family. He needed to stay for his wife and for her parents. It was his duty and responsibility, Peter continues as he finishes his sad tale.

Charley sits quietly as he speaks. She is mesmerized by his story, and his care and concern for his wife's family. She looks into his dark, brooding eyes, and goose bumps appear on her arms. His tale is just so poignant. She imagines him doting on his wife, taking care of her, and Charley's heart takes him in. They're both quiet for quite some time, each lost in their own thoughts when Peter finally breaks the silence and asks Charley about her last twenty-four years. She begins.

"Life has been good to me. I have five beautiful kids, who are the center of my world. It's been a pretty boring, standard life," she says.

But Peter wants to know more. He wants to know why she is so open to accepting his words of affection and his attention. And that is when the story she told Gayle comes spilling out. Only this time, there are no tears. Charley speaks with a quiet determination. She wants Peter to know about her life, but she doesn't want him to see her cry. After hearing his history, Charley realizes she has no right to cry. She finishes her tale with a half-hearted smile, hoping Peter will understand her motivations for getting involved with him.

Peter says "Ah, mia bella signora. You need a little attention."

"I have some," Charley replies with a smile playing across her face.

Peter picks up her hand, kissing her knuckles as he caresses her palm, sending shivers through her body. The spell is broken when the waitress appears with their sandwiches. She puts them down on the table and asks if they would like a refill on their drinks. Charley knows she needs to be careful, so she politely declines. Peter accepts the offer of one more beer, and with that, the waitress is off.

"Dig in, Bella. We have a long night ahead of us, and we need to keep our strength up," Peter declares picking up a portion of his giant muffaletta and devouring it bite by bite. Charley is stunned by the size of the sandwich placed in front of her. She begins to formulate a plan on how to eat it without appearing as ravenous as she really is.

* * *

With their lunches finished and most of Charley's sandwich packed up, the waitress stops by their table with the check. Charley, ever mindful of Gayle's words to her about becoming indebted to Peter, insists on paying for her portion.

"All right, Charley. I'll let you pay for yourself. But it goes against every grain of gentlemanliness I have in my body. I just don't want to see you upsetting yourself over something."

As Peter stands, he offers Charley his hand, and they walk to the car with their fingers loosely woven together. Releasing her hand, he helps her into the car and closes her door. The beauty of the car is not lost on Charley as she sits in the passenger seat. The engine roars to life with a mighty purr, and they're off to their hotel.

"Who will be there when we arrive?" Charley asks.

"Most everyone will be coming in throughout the night. David and Kristy are probably already checked in. The rest of the gang will go to dinner with us on Bourbon Street. I'm pretty sure Katherine's flight is the last one in. I think she told me she was sharing a room with you," Peter says.

"Yes, Katherine and I will share a room. Are you sharing with David?"

"No, I really don't like to share a room, so I have my own. Anyway, David is coming with Kristy, so obviously, they'll share a room," Peter responds.

A little thrill runs through Charley, followed by a jolt of panic, thinking what the heck would happen if she were alone in his room with him. She knows she needs to stay out of his room. It would be a scary place and one she's not sure she could emerge from unscathed. Charley needs to change the topic and get to safer footing, "I forgot that David and Kristy were coming together. Of course, they'd share a room." Charley continues on, "You told me we needed to eat to keep our strength up for tonight. What's on the agenda?"

"It's more like 'what's *not* on the agenda,' Charlene," Peter replies, "We're going to explore every nook and cranny of Bourbon Street—even places we would think of as 'taboo' at home, and we are going to have a ball."

Charley can just imagine all of them stepping into a fortune-teller's room. That would be hysterical. She's been once before, and it was funny to hear what these people, who have no idea who you really are, have to say about you. Remembering the first and only time she went to a tarot card reader on Bourbon Street, she smiles at the memory.

"What has put such a beautiful smile on your face?"

"Oh, I was just thinking about the time we went to a tarot card reader on Bourbon Street. It's just a lot of made-up stuff, but it was fun. It cracked us up for years." Charley continues on, "He was an older man who did all of our fortunes for us. He said I would be married by the time I was twenty-five. I would have two kids, and my husband would be a successful businessman. In other words, he told me what I wanted to hear. So, we played along for quite some time with his theory and got a lot of fun out of it. Of course, I wasn't married by the time I was twenty-five, so when that milestone came and went, I took a lot of teasing from my girlfriends. It cracks me up thinking there are people out there who say they can tell your story with cards."

Her laughter rang through the car as she finished, "I think we might have to add a tarot card reading into the night's events."

* * *

They pull up to the curb in front of the hotel, and the bellman comes to Charley's side of the car, helping her out. Peter hands the keys to the valet, and their bags are unloaded. They walk into the hotel and across the lobby hand in hand. Once they approach the registration desk, Peter withdraws his hand from Charley's, placing it on the small of her back as he propels her a little ahead of him. "I don't know if you'll be able to check into your room, yet. I think I remember Kate telling me it was reserved in her name only."

Charley begins to look a little frazzled until Peter says, "Let me check into my room, and you can put your things in there and even get ready to go out while we wait for Katherine to get here. No need to worry."

He knows Charley is nervous. He can sense her brain working overtime, wondering how to stay out of his room, but it looks like that won't be possible. He has her to himself.

"*Shit, shit, shit!*" Charley mutters under her breath, but she nods in agreement to the arrangement. She looks up to see a small smile spreading across Peter's face.

"Um, OK. I guess that will have to do for now. I really didn't plan this well, huh? I should have been the one to book the room since I was arriving earlier," Charley realizes.

"Well, then it's settled. The bellman can just bring your bag to my room, and we'll get ready to have a blast tonight," Peter announces, signaling the bellman to take Charley's bag.

He can almost feel Charley's heart begin beating a little faster as they get into the elevator taking them to his floor.

* * *

They approach the floor leading them to Peter's room. He feels her withdraw into herself a little. Charley's mood becomes very subdued. He quickly envelops her hand in his. "Bella, your hand is ice-cold. Let me warm them up for you a little," he offers, stroking her knuckles. In stark contrast to her hands, he sees the heat flaming her cheeks, and he feels small tremors of nerves coursing through her. He loves the feeling of power and control he has in the situation.

Peter cocks his head to one side as the elevator doors slide open saying, "Ah, Bella. No need to be nervous. I'm not going to bite you. We're just going to freshen up a bit." Charley gives Peter a small smile as they stop in front of the door to his room. The bellman quietly puts the bags inside and leaves with a generous tip in his hand. The door closes with a decided *thunk*.

At the sound of the door reverberating through the room, Charley jumps like a scared rabbit falling back into Peter who has come up very quietly from behind. He slowly places his hands on her shoulders and she freezes, rooted to her spot.

Peter knows he needs to proceed with caution, but he truly can't help himself. Charley's perfume is truly captivating. He leans down behind her, inhaling deeply as his nose gently caresses her neck. He can feel the goose bumps spring up on Charley's arms, and he knows she is reacting to his touch, to his proximity. He slowly turns her around and leans down to kiss her again. This kiss is gentle and sweet. He needs to lower her guard a little. He wants her in his collection more than he can ever remember wanting to add any woman. Charley leans into Peter's kiss, tilting her face upward. He feels the passion beginning to course through her, and he draws her closer. The ringing of a phone pulls Peter's attention from their kiss before the sound registers with Charley.

"Oh," she says shaking her head and pulling herself out of their embrace, "My internal alarm bells are going off. This isn't what I should be doing." Her face blanches white, and she says. "Oh, shit! It's not alarm bells at all. It's my phone!"

He can see the physical change come over her. Her mouth looks visibly parched; the remorse from their shared kiss is visible on her face. Charley reaches for her phone, "I need to check that. It could be from one of the kids."

7:45 p.m.

Hi Mom! I hope your flight was good. I miss you already, but I hope you have fun.

"Oh Noelle, what a sweetheart you are."

Peter watches the emotions roll through Charley; he thinks he can see her stomach do a little heave when she is brought back to reality.

Peter lifts her phone out of her hand and says, "Charlene, I can see that you're a little upset about our kiss, but we're adults. What's wrong with adults enjoying each other a little, especially if they like and trust each other? You do trust me, don't you, Bella?"

He watches her emotions play across her face. He senses that an answer to his question won't be so easy to find.

"Listen, Peter. I need to answer my daughter. And then, I think we should focus on getting ready to go out," Charley says, completely avoiding Peter's question. With that, Charley lifts her phone out of Peter's hand. She replies to Noelle's text and then opens her bag to get her outfit out for the night's festivities.

Suddenly, Charley stops and looks around, realizes they are in no ordinary room. Peter watches her face as she takes in the setup of the beautifully appointed, spacious suite. The colors of the room play off her eyes. And he enjoys seeing the effect her surroundings have on her as he takes in the opulence of the suite as well. The main room is decorated in soft yellows and golds. There is a small table with seating for four and a gorgeous living area with a golden-blue overstuffed couch. A small smile plays across Peter's lips while he watches Charley's head swing to the right and focus just beyond the bar, finding the bedroom completely separate from the rest of the room.

"Sweet Charlene. The color has returned to your cheeks. Are you really that relieved? I won't make you answer that question."

Peter knows he needs to take the intensity down a little to keep Charley moving in the direction he is pushing her to go. He wants to make sure she is ready for a weekend of fun, but he needs her to trust him. So he switches gears.

Opening his suitcase, he brings out his shower kit and announces, "I'm heading to the shower. But before I go, let's have a pre-celebratory cocktail," Peter continues, pointing at a bottle of wine on the bar to the right of him. *She thinks she's safe now, knowing the bed is not front and center, but what she doesn't realize is that there are plenty of other cozy places to play in this room.*

Peter sees that Charley's defenses have been lowered a bit. He knows she feels safe enough to accept a glass of wine. Peter pops the bottle open, pouring them each a generous serving as his phone vibrates loudly with an incoming text.

"Ah, Bella, it seems we are to be interrupted this evening by our phones. I need to check on this. We'll toast our time in New Orleans in a minute."

Peter's face lights up with a grin as he begins to respond to the text. He tells Charley that Hannah, Sarah, Becky, and Tina have all arrived at the airport and are catching a cab to the hotel. The girls tell him they will be there within the hour.

He responds to the text, reading out loud as he types, "Sounds great, ladies. Remember, we have a nine o'clock reservation at Emeril's."

After he finishes replying to the ladies, he raises his glass to Charley's, "Here's to New Orleans. May it be more than we both expected."

Their glasses clink as Peter catches Charley's eye. His eyes seem to smolder with a burning intensity as he lifts his glass to his lips, inhales the aroma, and takes a sip of his wine. Charley's actions mirror Peter's. Their toast to New Orleans is complete. Peter lowers his glass to the bar, leans down in Charley's ear, inhales her sweet fragrance, and whispers that it's time for him to take a shower.

Peter leaves Charley standing in the middle of the room. He imagines her mind racing as it begins to wrap itself around what possibilities are ahead. He wonders if she feels remorse or passion. He knows she hasn't been desired like this in a long time. They never are. The girls in his collection are a neglected group. His aim is to change that. Charley is different, though. She's a special case. Her naïveté makes her an innocent kind of sexy, which he believes could turn out to be far more powerful than anything he's had before.

He hears Charley open her suitcase and wonders what kind of outfit she has planned for the evening. He turns on the shower as he begins to get hard at the thought of her long, slim legs peeking out from beneath her skirt. He wants her, and he wants her now, but he knows it would be a mistake. He blasts the cold water to help ease his discomfort. He finishes his shower and steps out humming *Tuca Tuca*. He knows she can hear him; he smiles inwardly, reveling in the fact that he has such power over her emotions.

Peter emerges from the bathroom wrapped in a towel with his hair glistening from his shower. Charley stops dead in her tracks as she takes in the broad expanse of his shoulders and the narrowness of his waist. He has a smattering of dark hair covering his upper chest and tapering down into a happy trail, and he can tell from her reaction that Charley's thoughts are being led astray.

Watching her face carefully, Peter knows his physique is responsible for her reaction. He works hard to keep himself in shape, and it pays off when it comes to the women in his life. He watches the emotions play across Charley's face. He is tempted to walk over to her and kiss her until she surrenders, but then he sees the small shake of her head, and he knows she is trying to bring herself back to reality.

Charley's voice is soft, breathy when she tells Peter she needs to take a quick shower as well. Her words seem to catch in her throat as she passes Peter on her way to the bathroom.

"I won't take long. I just need to wash some of the travel off of me." As she passes him, he hears her sharp inhale when she gets a whiff of his freshly applied cologne. He watches her out of the corner of his eye, and he sees a slight hesitation before she forces herself to walk forward.

He looks at her suitcase and realizes her clothes for the evening are laid out, but forgotten. He wonders how she plans to solve this dilemma. No clean clothes. No bathrobe. He could easily help her out. The gentleman in him thinks he should take her clothes and leave them in front of the bathroom door. The rest of him knows exactly how he wants this to play out. He feels the slow burn of desire ignite when he picks up her dress, running his hands over the softness of the fabric. He can't wait to see her draped in a towel trying to get the garment from him. *Let's see how you handle this, little Bella.* Her shower is quick. His desire heightens. He is ready for her to appear. *Will you appear in your towel like I did, fighting fire with fire? Will you be brave enough? And if so, know I'm ready for you.* His pants begin to strain with his appendage growing larger at the thought of her.

She appears at the door, dressed only in a towel, just as he had hoped. Charley's shoulders are squared, her head is held high, but he can see the fear flitting behind her eyes when she sees Peter standing in the middle of the room holding the top she planned to wear in his hands.

"Ah, Bella. I figured you'd need this. You could have just asked me for it. I would have brought it to you," he says with smile playing across his lips.

Charley's face flames bright red, as he seems to read her mind. He knows that it's futile for her to fight fire with fire when she feebly asks him for her clothes.

"I'll give them to you on one condition. This is supposed to be a dress. Don't ruin it by putting leggings underneath. You have gorgeous legs, and they shouldn't be covered up by all this clothing."

Her dress is hanging from his fingertips. Charley reaches him much faster than he anticipated and grabs her top from his hand before he can react. He watches her walk to her suitcase with on trembling legs, feigning bravado. Charley takes her leggings and her undergarments, and stalks back to the bathroom to dress without saying a word.

A few minutes later, a calm Charley walks out of the bathroom in her dress and leggings. She picks up her glass of wine as she looks at Peter and says, "I appreciate the fact that you think my legs are nice, but it's a little chilly outside, and I like to stay warm. And besides, I'm not very good about having men tell me how to dress. I prefer to dress myself, thank you very much." Charley finishes forcefully. Peter discerns a change come over the beautiful, alluring woman standing in front of him as she takes control of her nerves.

* * *

Peter stands in stunned silence as he watches Charley's blue eyes turn from a soft, dark blue to deep, rich midnight color as she speaks. He feels the return of the uncomfortable tightening in his pants as he realizes how her fiery speech has affected him. He likes the sweet, innocent Charley a lot. But the woman who stands in front of him now, secure and confident is sexy as hell.

"All right, bella signora. I will not tell you how to dress. As I can see that you do more than a fine job of it yourself. You look breathtaking," Peter says as he takes in her full appearance.

Charley stands before him in her short, black sweater dress with dark-gray opaque tights underneath. They aren't quite leggings, but they aren't quite tights, either. They're slim and sleek with a hint of a pattern. They show off Charley's legs better than he could have ever imagined. Her legs being covered only add to the sexiness of her outfit. She has kept her cowboys boots on, and Peter's mind immediately envisions Charley standing at the foot of his bed wearing nothing but her boots. The tightening increases, and Peter finds himself trying hard to focus on the rest of Charley's appearance. Her hair is done in the same soft, wavy style it was when he picked her up. Her makeup has been taken up a notch with deep smoky eyes and soft pale lips. Charley has somehow managed to play up her gorgeous eyes even more. They stand out, making her appear doe eyed and innocent. That look, combined with the killer outfit, is a recipe Peter can't wait to sample.

She thinks she's won a small battle about her choice of clothing. But what she doesn't know is that she played right into my hand. Her confidence is ill founded. Maybe she thinks she is ready to take me on and win, but she is mistaken. This is my game, and I fully intend to be the victor.

Peter's phone sounds with a text tone, letting them know the rest of the girls have arrived and are ready to head to Emeril's for their reservation.

Peter turns to Charley, offers her his arm, and they leave the suite to go find the other girls.

* * *

When the elevator doors open to the lobby, Charley is stunned at the sight that greets her. She hadn't been paying much attention to her surroundings when they walked into the hotel earlier, and now Charley fully appreciates what a beautiful place it really is. The floors of the lobby are white-and-brown marble inlaid together giving the floor a warmth and brilliance that couldn't be achieved with just a stark, white marble. There are square, fluted columns holding up the vast ceiling, which is beautifully painted in soft greens and golds. The chandeliers are immense crystal light fixtures that seem to send sparks flying through the air as the lights reflect and bounce off each individual prism.

As they approach the center of the lobby, Charley sees her classmates sitting on a round couch talking excitedly to one another. Peter allows Charley's hand to drop to her side as they get closer and closer. He reaches their friends before she does and is immediately swallowed up in a sea of laughter, hugs, and kisses. Charley can't help but feel a pang of jealousy as he accepts embraces from all of the women standing before him.

Her conscience admonishes her for feeling even the slightest bit jealous. You have NO room to feel envy. You are married to another man. Peter is not yours!

Charley is brought into the fold as soon as the first round of hugs is delivered. Tina is the first to make sure Charley is properly greeted with a giant hug. And then all at once, Charley is in the middle of the mob of classmates with everyone talking excitedly around her.

Charley's jealousy soon fades as the group heads out the door to Emeril's restaurant, each person peppering her with questions about how she's been, how her kids are, and what she's doing now, as they head to the restaurant. The four girls all still live in Ann Arbor, so they're familiar with each other's lives, kids, and jobs. Peter makes it back to Ann Arbor often for holidays and games, and his whole family still lives there, making it a good draw for him. So he, too, is up to date on the lives of these four women. Charley's parents moved to Florida several years ago, so there is not much to bring her back to the place she used to call home. Charley's home is now Louisville, and although Ann Arbor seems a world far removed from her, she finds comfort and instant camaraderie with her old friends.

The group heads out the door to the restaurant in high spirits. Their laughter and joviality echo through the crisp night March air. Peter is leading the group to their destination. He is in deep conversation with Tina, and Charley can't help but wonder what the two could be talking about with their heads bent together as they walk. Charley is hanging toward the back listening to Hannah explain why it was so important for her to stay in Ann Arbor after she finished college. Charley finds herself paying only a little bit of attention to her because she is straining to hear what Peter and Tina could possibly be talking about.

Arriving at the restaurant, Peter drops back to Charley's side. When they are seated, he makes sure to find his place next to her. All of the friends begin to study the menu, and Charley is stunned to see the choices. None of them look low-calorie or healthy, and after today's lunch, she is well aware of how much she's consumed, including the whiskey and wine. She sits and mulls her selection carefully until she feels a heat searing in her leg as Peter's thigh brushes hers.

Her senses are on overdrive now. She can barely see the menu, and her worries about calories seem to head out the window as the waiter approaches their table. Tina orders first, choosing the Andouille-crusted drum. After the others choose their meals, it's Charley's turn.

Surprising herself, she hears her voice say, "I'd like the filet mignon, please," figuring if she is going to throw caution to the wind this weekend, she might as well start with her food choices.

With dinner winding down and the wine supply drying up, the group decides it's time to leave so they can experience everything New Orleans has to offer. They pay their bill, thank their waiter, and head out to explore the festivities of Bourbon Street.

Knowing it's more of a hike than the girls would prefer, Peter decides to call a couple of taxis. The hostess is more than happy to assist their group and calls the local cab company asking for a van to come get the group. As soon as the van shows up, they pile in, and off they go to continue their fun for the night.

They ask the cabbie to drop them near The Blacksmith on Bourbon Street so they can get a famous, albeit not Pat O'Brien's, hurricane. They pay the fare, tipping the cabbie generously.

The driver hands Peter his business card, wishing them a good night, "Call me any time you need a good, reliable driver. My name is Cedric. I'm your man."

They thank him for his time and say they will definitely need his services during the weekend. They wave good-bye and head toward their first, of hopefully many, hurricanes.

Peter leads them to The Blacksmith Bar, telling the girls their hurricanes are much better than Pat O'Brien's. They walk in, order a drink to go and begin their night meandering down one of the most famed streets in the United States. "All right, ladies, I know I've asked most of you this question, but let me just sell it a little more. Marie Laveau's House of Voodoo is a mere three-minute walk from here. With her knowledge, her insight, and a few bills slipped into her palm, she'll be able to tell you what fabulous and exciting adventures are in your future. So, let's see, who's in?" and he is rewarded with a resounding cheer of approval from all of the ladies in his company.

Drinks in hand, the six friends find themselves in the sanctuary of the voodoo shop. "Even though you were all in favor of this just a few minutes ago, I can see no one wants to go first. I'll be the gentleman and break the ice for you all."

One by one, the group is seated at a table, and their cards are pulled ... past, present, and future. They all ooh and aah at the appropriate places in their readings; each of them seems satisfied with his or her tarot card time. It is finally Charley's turn, and she finds herself a bit nervous and shaky. She doesn't remember feeling scared or intimidated the first time she had a tarot card reading, but for some reason, this time feels different.

When she sits down at the table, the reader looks directly into her eyes and says quietly so only Charley can hear her, "I can feel your energy. You have an angry and confused air about you. Let's see what the cards have to say."

The first card is drawn and left face down on the table in the past position. Charley draws her next card, and as she does, the reader says, "This is your future card."

Realizing her mistake in calling the next card the future card instead of Charley's present card, the reader places the next card in the future position. Charley then pulls her third and final card, placing it in the present position. The reader turns over the first card, which is the Four of Wands. The second card is turned over, revealing the Lovers. Finally, the third card is presented in the future position. The Five of Cups occupies the final spot.

Charley does not understand the meaning behind each of these cards, but something tells her she desperately needs to grasp and hold onto what is being said to her. The reader's words are not processing in her head. Charley is trying hard to focus on what she is saying, but nothing makes sense. She looks up in confusion, beginning to realize that the alcohol has finally done its job and completely dulled her senses. Somehow, she manages to make the reader understand that she needs to buy a book so she can read and reread everything she is hearing.

The reader, having seen many intoxicated people in the store, takes Charley to the front, places a book in her hands, and leads her to the register so she can pay for it. "This is the first time I have done this," she whispers. "I'm marking all three of the cards you pulled. Please read the notes when you are able to understand. Your anger and confusion are overwhelming you. This will help."

Charley's brain is a muddled mess. She knows she needs to go to bed. The time for fun has passed. Her alcohol limit was reached before the hurricane, and now she is quickly declining.

"Charley, it's time to take you home. You need a little time to recuperate and rest. I'll take you back to the hotel and get you settled in," Peter says, turning to the others in their party. "Once I have her safely tucked in, I'll come back out and find you all. Now, let's give Cedric a call." Charley leans on Peter for support. It is time to get back to the hotel.

When the taxi arrives, Peter piles Charley inside. She presses her face up against the window to try and cool down the boiling in her head and stomach. Peter takes her hand and reassures her he will take care of her, as Cedric carefully navigates the streets of New Orleans. "Oh, man. I'll get you back quickly. I've seen this scenario a few times here." He looks at Peter and says, "The last thing we need is to have her lose it in the cab. It's no good for you, and it's terrible for my business. Let's roll," he states as Charley slumps into the back seat. She feels herself being pulled from the back seat and watches Peter reach for his wallet. With glazed eyes and slurred speech, she manages, "Here, let me pay the nice, nice cab man." Charley misses the look of amusement that passes between Cedric, Peter, and the bellman who has come to help her inside.

"Man, you got your work cut out for you tonight, don't ya?" Cedric asks Peter as the bellman helps Charley through the front door.

"Yeah, this isn't exactly how I envisioned the evening's end," Peter mutters as he lays a big tip in Cedric's hand. "Thanks for getting us back safe and sound. We have a big night tomorrow night, too. Hopefully, we'll see you then."

Once Peter is inside with Charley, he takes over for the bellman and begins to walk toward the elevator with Charley propped up under his arm. They reach the elevator doors, step inside, and Peter hits the button at the same time Charley realizes she doesn't have a room.

Looking up at Peter with glazed eyes, she tries hard not to slur her words, "I need to get a room. I know I can't scheck into Katherine's room, but I need to get a room. Can you pleassssse take me to the front deshk?"

The elevator doors close as Charley finishes her question. She reaches for the open door button but is too late. The elevator begins its journey up to Peter's suite. Charley's brain is beginning to process and rebel at the thought of going to his room.

She starts to fight with Peter a bit until he says, "There is no need to worry, little Bella. I will put you to bed for now, and when Katherine gets to the hotel, I will move you to her room. You are so drunk right now, there is no way I would consider taking advantage of you. I only want you when you're lucid. I want you to feel every sensation I give you."

Charley relaxes a bit, knowing Peter will be true to his word. At the same time, though, she realizes exactly what Peter just said, and a tingle runs through her.

She tries to look up coyly at Peter and suggests, "Well, we could jusht try a little tonight to see if I can feel anysthing."

"Ah sweet Bella, the alcohol is talking for you now. It's time for you to go to bed and sleep this off."

Peter has Charley firmly around the waist as he opens the door to his suite. No sooner is the door open, than Charley excuses herself to the bathroom. Peter can only hope she is going to empty her stomach of the alcohol swimming within. He appears at the door, holding two bottles of water. Charley's stomach is violently trying to rid her system of the hurricane and the wine. She looks up to see him standing in the doorway of the bathroom and asks him to please get out. "Your wish is my command," he says, complying with her request and leaving the bottles of water on the sink for her.

After what feels like an eternity to Charley, her stomach finally seems to be rid of its contents. Sitting down gingerly on the bathroom floor, she reaches up for a bottle of water and takes a small sip. With the toilet flushed and her face washed, Charley walks out into the living room to face Peter. Although she is still intoxicated, she realizes she must look like a complete moron to him for getting so inebriated, and she sits down next to him to try and explain.

"I don't drink much." Charley is trying hard not to slur her words. She goes on to tell him, "I only drink wine, and I never mix my alcohol."

Peter brushes away her concerns about making a fool of herself, while he pushes her hair out of her eyes. "Listen, it's no big deal. We've all done it. Just go to sleep, and I'll make sure you're taken care of tonight. Drink your water," he says before standing up to get her some ibuprofen. "Tonight will be tough, but tomorrow might not be so bad if you drink your water and rehydrate."

Peter comes back to the couch just as Charley's eyes are closing. "Charlene. You need to take these," he commands placing the ibuprofen in her hands and making her take a sip of water so she can swallow the pills. "Bella, Bella, Bella, this is not exactly the way I wanted tonight to go. But I will get to have you in my bed," he says carrying Charley into his room and tucking her into the large bed in the middle of the bedroom.

CHAPTER EIGHT

CHARLEY WAKES UP the next morning with a splitting headache and no idea of where she is. She opens her eyes, taking in the sights that greet her.

It hits her all at once. Oh God, I'm in Peter's room!

She peeks under the covers to see if she is dressed, thanking her lucky stars that she is in her jammies. Looking to her side again, she thanks her stars that the opposite side of the bed is empty and seems like it hasn't been slept in. Charley sits up quickly and immediately regrets the action. She slumps back into the pillows with a groan. She gently opens her eyes again and spots the large bottle of water on the nightstand with four tablets of ibuprofen beside it.

Somebody was looking out for me last night.

Reaching out for the water and the medicine, Charley greedily drinks, hoping a small miracle will stop the throbbing in her head.

She glances at the clock and sees that it's only seven in the morning. She closes her eyes and is rewarded with another two hours of sleep.

The next time her eyes open, it's to the sounds of water running in the bathroom, letting her know Peter is in the shower. She sits up gently, feeling much better, and famished. She knows she needs to get some food in her soon if she has any hope of staving off a massive hangover. As she sits in bed, she can't believe how stupid she had been yesterday. She knows better than to mix different types of alcohol together. If she had just stayed with the wine at dinner, she would have been fine.

But no, you had to go and add that damn hurricane.

Knowing that self-recriminations won't do anything to help ease her hangover, Charley slides out of bed as the water from the shower is turned off.

Peter walks into the living room and states with a mischievous grin, "Well, well, well. Look who finally decided to join the land of the sober. I'm glad you're up, but I have to say, I'm a little disappointed. I walk into the shower with you tucked safely in my bed, and I come out to an empty bed. I was thinking I would join you."

Charley flushes crimson not only at his teasing remark, but also at the sight of him. Before she can say a word, Peter cuts her off saying, "Ah, Bella. Please don't worry about a thing. I am teasing you. I wouldn't climb into bed with you. Please don't worry about your behavior last night. We all understand. Every one of us has done it before."

Charley is beginning to feel better about what happened until Peter continues, "It's OK and actually kind of understandable. You barely ate a thing yesterday. Your sandwich is in the fridge with nothing but a couple of bites missing. And at dinner, you only ate a tiny portion of your meal. If you're going to drink like you did yesterday, you have to eat as well," he chides.

Charley's face grows hot again, and it is up to Peter to soothe her. "Please don't worry, but *please*, for the love of God, *eat* today if you're going to drink! I'll fill you in on our plans for the day, as soon as I'm dressed and you're showered," Peter tells.

Charley rises, sheepishly, from the couch knowing Peter is right and truly regretting her behavior last night. As she passes him, though, he pinches her ass and laughs, "I have to say you were mighty sexy sleeping all alone in that big bed of mine."

She smacks his arm as he tries to grab for her again and races toward the bathroom to wash the stench of alcohol and vomit from her body.

Charley is freshly showered and clothed in another set of pajamas. She sits down on the couch and begins to brush through her hair while Peter tells her the plans for the day.

* * *

Before he can begin, there is a knock at the door. A muffled voice from the other side calls out "room service," and Peter gets up to bring their breakfast in. Charley's mouth waters as the smell of bacon and syrup wafts through the air. The server places their breakfast on the table and quietly leaves them alone after accepting a generous tip from Peter.

They abandon their places on the couch and sit down to eat. Charley is famished and very thankful Peter had ordered food for her. She digs into bacon, eggs, and toast, remembering from her college days it was this kind of combination that would help settle her stomach and give her a good base to carry her through the day.

As they eat, Peter fills her in on their plans. They are going to take it easy and just hang out at the rooftop pool for some much-needed relaxation. And then, around four, they will all go back to their rooms to get ready to delve into more of Bourbon Street before finding a restaurant for dinner.

Charley is ready to relax a little and enjoy some quiet time before heading out to explore again. They finish their breakfast in companionable silence, with no seductive or suggestive comments from Peter.

Charley has to admit she likes the calm Peter better than the Peter on the prowl. He is good company and easy to be around. When he's in his predatory mode he is a bit scary and more than Charley can handle. She feels like he sucks the air out of her and keeps her off balance when he comes onto her.

With breakfast finished, Charley heads to the bathroom with her bathing suit in hand, at Peter's request. He tells her he wants her to take it easy, so he will clean up from breakfast. On her way to the bathroom, Charley sees the book she bought from the tarot card reader, and she makes a mental note to take it to the pool. She wants to remember what the woman told her last night as the wave of inebriation was sweeping over her.

Charley emerges from the bathroom in her bathing suit and cover-up to find Peter standing in the bedroom shirtless and already in his swimming trunks. Charley gives an audible gasp at the sight of him standing there with his broad shoulders rippling in the sunlight that is coming in through the curtains.

She knows he hears her because a wicked grin creeps across his face as he tries to tempt her, "You know, my sweet, delicious friend, we could just stay in this lovely suite of mine and find our own entertainment for the day."

Charley is astounded. She spent the better part of last night barfing in front of this gorgeous man standing two feet away from her, and he's still coming onto her.

With a laugh, Peter continues, "I can see by the look on your face you need a little relaxation at the pool and not calisthenics in bed."

Charley grabs her book as Peter takes her hand, and they head up to the rooftop pool. Before the elevator opens, the two drop hands as their friends' laughter echoes through the doors. The group has now grown to include all of their high school friends. Hugs are dispensed as Charley is caught up to date on what happened last night after she was taken home. She suffers a bit of well-deserved ribbing at her state of intoxication from the night before, but she takes it all in stride.

As they step out of the elevator at the rooftop level, Charley's eyes take a moment to adjust to the watery brightness of the late winter sunlight. She is feeling better, but the extreme light of the day combined with the boisterous voices of those around her makes her jumpy. She knows she needs to relax if she is going to make it through another two nights of partying. They walk toward their lounge chairs, and the warmth of the pool deck surprises Charley. When she was checking out the hotel online before heading to New Orleans, she read about how the temperature on the roof feels so much warmer in winter months because the heat from the pool is trapped by the glass walls enclosing the roof top. She wasn't sure she believed what she had read, but now with the sun beating down, no chill, and seeing the gorgeous layout in front of her, she's excited to know it's true. As Charley begins to relax in the balmy air, her plan begins to solidify and she looks forward to claiming a lounge chair while reading in the warmth of the sun.

Walking toward their chairs, Katherine appears beside Charley, with a conspiratorial whisper, "I'm sorry about you not being able to get into our room last night, but I'm sure you had a wonderful time in Peter's room."

Charley stammers, "Oh, my gosh, it so wasn't like that at all. I puked and then passed out. I don't think I could have moved if I tried."

Coming to Charley's rescue, Peter says to Katherine with the ease of old, close friends, "Some people aren't as well trained as you and can't do what you do. I think Charley could benefit from your lessons."

Charley doesn't know what to make of their conversation, so she busies herself by getting her chaise lounge set up and comfortable. She puts herself on the periphery of the group, choosing a chair next to David and Kristy. She pulls off her cover-up, and as she begins to bend over to sit down, she feels a shiver run down her spine as Peter's voice quietly caresses her from behind.

"Oh Bella, I knew your body was beautiful, but I had no idea it was *this* beautiful," he remarks as he runs his index finger down her back.

Charley is relieved she has sunglasses on because she's sure her eyes would have given away the effect Peter's touch has on her as she collapses into her lounge chair, hoping no one else has noticed their exchange.

Once everyone gets settled into their chairs, an afternoon of relaxing begins. Charley pulls out her tarot card book, as all of the friends either break into small groups of conversation, or pull out a book of their own. Charley is looking forward to exploring the world of tarot cards as she soaks up the rays and enjoys some downtime. She opens the book, and her three tarot cards spill into her lap. A card with four tall poles is the first one out. She is not at all familiar with tarot cards and their meanings, but for some reason, she has a feeling that she needs to understand them. The next card she picks up is a person in a black cloak with, what looks to be, five chalices on the ground at their feet. Her third card says on the bottom, the Lovers. That one seems pretty self-explanatory, so she digs into the first two.

Charley flips through the pages until she finds what she's looking for as Kristy asks her what she's reading. Charley explains that they went to a tarot card reader last night, but she was too intoxicated to absorb what the reader was saying, so she bought a book to fill in where the tarot card reader's words became unclear. She and Kristy sit together, pouring over the contents, with Kristy interjecting now and again, trying to help Charley decipher the world of tarot cards.

Charley reads out loud.

"With the Four of Wands in the past position, effort and commitment were used sagely to build a foundation upon which you are standing. The Four of Wands can also foretell a coming surprise when this card is in anything but the past position. In the past position, however, this card shows a wonderful payout of living a life of joy."

The girls go on to read about card combinations, seeing which cards affect others and find out that when the Lovers card is pulled at the same time as the Four of Wands, it can mean that the man in your life is going to pop the question. Charley's heart flutters a little bit, wondering what kind of question awaits her. She looks up to find Peter staring right at her and is again thankful for her sunglasses. Instead of feeling conspicuous, Charley feels a small amount of confidence as she raises her water bottle to him as she and Kristy go on to read more about the remaining two tarot cards.

The person in the black cloak with the five chalices at his feet, according to the book, represents the Five of Cups. The card brings a feeling of sadness to Charley, and part of her wants to skip this card, but she knows she can't. She needs to find out why she is feeling this way. The figure on the card is standing with his face turned away and his back facing out. The sky around the lone figure is gray and dull. There are three cups, which have been turned over, spilling their contents, and the scene in front of her makes Charley uncomfortable and edgy. Last night, Charley pulled this card in the future position. She begins to read and immediately knows this card is speaking to her.

"There are a few cards in the deck responsible for breaking bad news. If you ask most tarot card readers their feelings on the Five of Cups, they will tell you they don't see it as an upsetting event. If this card is drawn, the person receiving the reading already knows of his or her sorrow and loss. This is the card confirming things are a little off kilter in a person's life."

Charley knows all too well that her life is not as she had envisioned for herself. It is a sad and angry place when it comes to Garrett and their marriage. Not wanting to dwell on the sadness, Charley puts the Five of Cups quietly to the side, moving on to dig into the next card.

Even to Charley's untrained eye, she can see the meaning behind the naked woman standing under a serpent-wrapped tree and the man standing in front of a tree of flames. The significance is there. She knows it's the temptation of Eve, and she realizes she should apply it to this flirtation with Peter. But it feels so good to be looked at and thought of as sexy. She doesn't want to give up this feeling, so Charley delves deeper into the interpretation of the card before she lets her conscience rule the day. Charley skips to the part where the book tells her what she wants to hear.

"When the location of the card is in the present position, your passions for a new romance are palpable. If this card is drawn in the present position, it will end loneliness in a hurry. Whether you know your romantic partner or not is irrelevant. What is relevant, however, is the influence and impact you both will have on each other in all aspects of your lives. You will reshape each other. There will be a definitive line where you will be able to look back on your present day and see a before and an after effect of how you transformed each other."

Charley hands the book to Kristy, who has become more and more intrigued as she has gotten pulled further into the page on the Lover's card.

Charley didn't know Kristy well in high school, but she has gotten closer with her since she has seen her regularly at reunions. Except for Peter, Kristy and Katherine are the two in this group she knows the best. Charley feels a comfortable silence fall between them as Kristy reads the tarot card book, and Charley tries to take in the words she has read. What she believes she has deciphered seems to be pointing her down a path with Peter. The Lovers.

Why was that pulled if she wasn't supposed to fall into a romance with him, especially if you couple it with the Four of Wands card in the past position? If she believes the cards, Peter is going to ask her some kind of question. She just doesn't know what yet.

And then she has the Five of Cups card in the future position. It shows that her life is sad and meaningless. *But it doesn't have to be,* the little voice in Charley's head reminds her. *You could easily add some spice and excitement to your life. Peter wants you. You know he does. All you have to do is say the word, and he'll be yours.*

At that moment, Charley looks up to see Peter's brown eyes languidly looking over every inch of her. A jolt of excitement shoots through her as she formulates a plan for the evening. Kristy's voice breaks through Charley's reverie, ending the fantasy world she stirred up and bringing her back to the present. "Thanks for letting me read your book, Charley. I think I'm going to have to go experience a tarot card reader and see what they have to say about my past, present, and future. I'm going to make David take me there tonight!"

Charley looks up to see a few in the group starting to pack up their pool bags. They are beginning to head back down to their rooms to start getting ready for the evening. Charley looks over at Katherine who is walking toward her.

"Hey, Charley, I'm going to pop down to our room to start getting ready. Here's a key for whenever you want to come in," she tells her.

Charley takes the key saying, "I'll just go down to Peter's room and pack up my stuff. I'll give you time to shower, and then I'll be in to do the same!"

Katherine walks to where Peter is sitting, leans over him, giving him a nice view of her ample cleavage and whispers in his ear as she and Peter both look at Charley. As Katherine stands up, Peter does the same. Katherine saunters toward the elevators and waves goodbye to the group. Peter packs his things up and walks to Charley with a key, offering, "Come down whenever you'd like, little Bella. I'll help you take your things to Katherine's room."

Charley can hear Katherine's voice call out to Peter, telling him the elevator is there, and with that, he leaves. Charley has no idea what their exchange was about but feels a twinge of anxiety and jealousy mix together in the pit of her stomach. She has doesn't understand why, but she just feels something is brewing between Peter and Katherine.

Charley sits quietly for a few more minutes chatting with Kristy and David about their lives back at home. Charley fills them both in on her kids and her job. She sits and marvels at how they connect with each other. Theirs is an easy, sweet marriage. Kristy is lying on her lounge chair in the middle of them all. David is sitting facing her and Charley, and they bring each other up to date. While they are talking, Charley can feel the love flowing between them. They are completely in tune with each other, and Charley is in awe of how they make their love seem so easy. She watches their interactions. They work so well together. To Charley, they effortlessly make each other feel they are the center of the other's world.

After chatting for a while longer, David takes Kristy's hand and announces, "All right, babe. It's time to get you ready to go out. You're going to be one smoking hot mama tonight, strolling down Bourbon

Street, and you're all mine. I can't wait to show you off, but first, it's shower time." They start packing up, and Charley is left alone on the pool deck, feeling a little unsettled but excited about the night.

* * *

Charley puts her cover-up on, packs up her pool bag, and walks slowly toward the elevators. She pushes the button for Peter's floor and turns toward his room, feeling unsettled. She takes out the key card he gave her and lets herself in. She can hear the water running and is shocked at how relieved she feels. She knows now she won't have to be alone with him, even though the plan she formulated this afternoon had everything to do with trying to be alone with Peter. Seeing how he interacted with Katherine set off an alarm. Charley doesn't know why, she just knows something has been altered.

Quickly packing her bag, she is relieved to see she had kept her toiletries together. She hasn't left anything in the bathroom. Charley zips up her suitcase as she hears the water turn off. She leaves the key on the table, takes her bag, and leaves for Katherine's room on the eighth floor.

Not wanting to startle Katherine, Charley knocks lightly on the door to the room she will now be sharing with her. Hearing no response, Charley inserts her key card into the lock, opens the door, calling out, "Hey, Katherine. I'm here now."

There is still no response from Katherine, so Charley knocks lightly on the bathroom door. As she does, the door swings open, revealing only emptiness. Hmmm, that's odd, I wonder where she is.

Charley can tell Katherine has already showered. The bathtub is wet, and there are towels hanging on the shower rod. Charley looks at the clock as she walks further into the room and sees how late it is. She hadn't realized she stayed at the pool so much longer than everyone else. As she puts her bag on one of the beds, she sees a note from Katherine. "Hey Charley. Went to grab a cocktail. Get your ass moving so we can get out and party!"

Charley wastes no time getting ready. She showers, applies her makeup, and unpacks her outfit in record time. She is in the midst of finishing her hair when Katherine walks into the room with a cocktail in hand for her.

"Hey, slowpoke," Katherine says, as she puts the drink down on the bathroom counter, "we're all waiting for you."

"I'm almost ready," Charley answers, cautiously picking up the glass and being pleasantly surprised at the lack of recoil from her stomach as she takes the first sip of the fruity rum punch. "I didn't realize how long I stayed up at the pool. I was chatting with David and Kristy, and then once they left, I just lost track of time."

Charley puts the finishing touches on her appearance and walks out of the bathroom. Katherine emits a low whistle and says, "Wow! Look at you. A little hottie! You're gonna be turning heads tonight."

"Oh, my gosh," Charley responds. "Thank you, but I think *you're* the one who's going to be the head-turner tonight! You look smokin'!"

A touch of envy spreads through Charley as she takes in Katherine's appearance. Killer curves are highlighted under her leggings and swingy green top with a dramatic, plunging neckline accentuating her flawless bustline. She is perfectly proportioned without an ounce of fat. Looking at Katherine makes Charley feel a little self-conscious as she stands there in a tailored red jacket, skinny black jeans, and cowboy boots. Compared to Katherine, Charley looks like she is going to work, not out on the town in New Orleans. *Oh, well,* she laments inwardly, *there's not much I can do at this point. This is the outfit I brought, and I'm not sexy like Katherine.*

"Charley, Charley, Charley," Katherine says, as if reading her mind. "You are one stunning lady. I can't believe you haven't noticed that yet. With all of Peter's attention, I thought he would have driven that point home by now."

Charley's face flushes as she processes what Katherine has just said. "Oh my God! You noticed? Do you think everyone else noticed, too?" Charley is too flustered to pretend that nothing has gone on with Peter.

"Oh, honey," Katherine reassures her, "don't worry about a thing. I think I'm the only one who noticed how attentive he is of you. Now, let's get going. They're all waiting for us in the lobby." Katherine grabs both of their purses. "Come on! It's time to go have some fun!

Katherine and Charley appear in the lobby just as the rest of the group is coming out of the bar. Peter takes one look at both girls together and lets out a long, low whistle. "Well, I think David and I are going to be the two luckiest guys in all of New Orleans tonight. We've got one gorgeous group of women with us!" Peter says ushering the group out the door and into the night air.

* * *

Peter falls into step with Charley as they head outside. Cedric and his oversized cab are waiting for them, along with another car. Peter holds Charley back and allows all of their friends to pile into the van. With Cedric's van full, Charley realizes Peter's plan was for them to have the car to themselves. Charley tries to stay calm. Her nerves are on edge. The meaning of the tarot cards plays through her mind, as does the scene with Peter and Katherine on the roof. There was something deeper to their conversation and to the fact that they left together, but Charley can't put a finger on what it might have been.

Charley fights her warring emotions as Peter tells their friends they'll meet them on Bourbon Street. With mounting tension building inside of her, Charley watches Cedric's van pull away from the curb. Through the open van window, she can hear Cedric say her name. She assumes he is asking the group how she's feeling today after being in such rough shape last night. Peter's hand is at her elbow, steering her toward their waiting cab. Helping Charley into the car, he then slides in effortlessly beside her.

Peter's hand covers Charley's as he compliments her, "You look beautiful tonight, little Bella. But I wish you'd lose the jacket. The sparkly top underneath would look much sexier without all the clothing covering it up. You are one sexy lady," he adds.

Charley's guard is being lowered by his sweet flattery, and she knows it. She can feel Peter leaning in closer to her as she whispers, "You know I don't like men telling me how to dress."

Peter's voice brushes against her ear, "You don't like a man telling you how to dress, so how would you like it if I told you I'd like to undress you?"

Charley's stomach flips as her world tilts a little. This is it. Tonight there is no turning back. She knows it now. There is no pretense anymore.

Charley finally lets herself grasp the fact that she is on the verge of a full affair with Peter. His magical words and flattery have won her over. Leaning into him, she accepts his kiss. Their lips search and sear against each other. Charley's mind shuts down, surrendering to the sensations racing around her body. Peter's lips leave hers, traveling down her neck, and sending shock waves of pleasure rippling through her.

"My God, sweet Bella. You are intoxicating." He begins to hum the tune from *Tuca Tuca* against her neck.

"When I look at you, I know what I want from you." Peter quotes the lyrics from the song as the cab pulls to a stop and brings Charley back down to earth.

Peter pays the cabbie as Charley catches sight of their friends disappearing into a store. Charley looks up at Peter as he suggests, "Why don't we join our friends?"

They walk to the store side by side, not holding hands, but their bodies brush against each other. The electricity between them sends little jolts of pleasure through Charley. As they get closer to the store, Charley can see what kind of a shop it is. *My friends have lost their minds*, she thinks to herself. They have all gone into a sex shop together.

"Holy shit!" Charley exclaims. "What are we doing?"

Taking her arm, Peter steers her into the shop, trying to be casual, "It's just for fun. Have a look around. You might find something you'd like to try."

Charley cannot believe she's going into a adult toy store, let alone going in with friends. She looks up at the sign above the door "Hustler Hollywood, huh?" she says as Peter opens the door for her.

"Yep, this is Larry Flint's Hustler Hollywood. It's one of the few sex shops in New Orleans where we can all go. Most of the others are a little too rough to take you girls into," Peter confidently explains.

Charley can hear Katherine and Tina laughing at something they've found. She looks around and is pleasantly surprised. The shop is light and clean. The other shoppers aren't walking around with their heads down in shame, she notices. The clerks are answering questions for them and pointing the way to other areas that might be of interest. The rest of the girls have gathered around an area of vibrators on a table. Charley leaves Peter's side, figuring it will be safer to explore a sex shop with girls than with Peter.

She walks up to the group as Katherine picks up the biggest vibrator on the table. Tina is holding one that is rotating around, swirling little beads at the bottom. Hannah has a long slender vibrator in her hands. The girls are all talking about the pros and cons of each toy. Charley has never been inside a sex shop before, so for her to see everyone handling these toys so casually leaves her feeling a little off-kilter. She looks up to see Peter watching her with a wicked grin. Trying to seem like she is at ease, Charley picks up an interesting-looking vibrator off the table. It is long and purple with a ring at the bottom. She has no idea what the ring is for, when Hannah pipes up, "Oh, I love the open ring at the bottom. It makes it more comfortable to use."

Charley can't believe all of these people know about these toys and how to use them. This is something she and her friends never discuss at home. She feels like she's been transported into a parallel universe as everyone keep on talking about the various toys in their hands and which ones they should buy. She puts the vibrator down and walks toward the clothing section, thinking that might be a safer area.

Charley sees David and Kristy walking hand-in-hand looking at various toys together and has to wonder what it would be like to walk through a store like this with someone who would want to buy and use these kinds of devices with her.

She can sense Peter is behind her before she hears his voice in her ear. "I bought something I think you might like to try later," he says with a deep, gravelly purr sending a thrill coursing through her veins.

She turns to look at Peter who is standing there with a small package in his hands. She knows she should be mortified, but instead, she feels a bit heady at the thought of someone buying something in a sex shop with her in mind. She watches David and Kristy as they make their way to the cash register, and a little pang of envy springs up in her chest, startling her. They are buying something to use together, exactly what she had just envisioned for herself a few minutes before. In that snapshot of a moment, Charley feels more than a bit queasy, knowing a man who is not her husband bought her something he thinks she might like to use from a sex shop.

The friends all begin to reconvene, some with bags in their hands and others, like Charley, empty handed. Kristy and David tell the group they want to go to the tarot card place. Everyone else but

Katherine has already been there, and it wasn't a place they needed to see twice. Hannah, Tina, Becky, and Sarah decide they want to go to the Cat's Meow for a little karaoke, drinking, and dancing. Charley is standing next to Peter when she sees a look pass between him and Katherine. Peter says he wants Katherine and Charley to come with him to this new club he's been hearing about. The proximity to Peter does things to Charley's head. She can't seem to think straight when he's near. One minute she's ready to dive headfirst into an affair, and the next, she thinks she might throw up because he bought something in a sex shop.

Who knows what it is? that little voice in her head asks. *He could have bought you a coffee cup as a joke, so just lighten up, and don't freak out.*

With everyone's plans made, Peter, Charley, and Katherine head off to Cedric's cab. Peter had the forethought to call him while they were all browsing in Hustler Hollywood. Charley and Peter are in the third row with Katherine sitting in the middle seat as Cedric puts the car in drive.

"Where to, ladies and gentlemen?" Cedric asks.

"We're off to the Jasmine Club, Cedric," Peter answers. "But first, we need to stop and pick up a couple of nice bottles of champagne."

"Ah, you're looking for a *good* night then, aren't you?" Cedric continues.

"Yes, I think it's going to be one night in a million," Peter replies as his fingers draw lazy circles on Charley's thigh.

Charley can feel an intensity in the car that she can't quite explain, but she knows there is something different in the air. It's as if everyone else knows something she doesn't. After their quick detour to the liquor store, the van stops in front of a nondescript three-story building. Katherine gets out first with Peter close behind. Peter then offers Charley his hand as she climbs out of the back seat.

They walk into the front of the club where Peter and Katherine show their membership cards. Peter tells the front desk he has a guest for the night, and he'll be paying her fee. He also lets them know that another gentleman will be joining them in the large group room.

Peter bends down to say something Charley can't quite hear, but she catches the words "private room." They enter the club and make their way to a room with two couches and a bar area. Peter pulls out the two bottles of champagne, along with a bottle of Basil Hayden's bourbon. He tells the girls they will first toast to the evening, and then he will make them Basil Fizzes to keep them in party mode all night.

Peter uncorks the champagne, pouring a generous amount in each glass.

The friends raise their glasses as Peter toasts, "To old friends, new experiences, and a night of fun."

Charley's stomach does a little flip-flop when Peter's eyes meet hers. It's almost as if he can read her thoughts. She begins to imagine what kind of fun they may have tonight when they get back to the hotel. Part of her knows she should run fast the other way, but his presence is wreaking havoc on her decision-making powers. She is under a spell whenever he stands so close to her. Peter and Katherine toss back their champagne as Charley takes a sip. It's now that Charley notices a tall blonde man walking into the room. For a minute, she thinks her eyes are playing tricks on her.

The man walking toward them looks a little like Garrett, and Charley begins to panic until Peter puts his hand out to the newcomer and greets him, "Welcome, Jeff. It's been too long." Peter makes the introductions and begins to prepare the Basil Fizzes he had promised.

Charley is pleasantly surprised by the flavor. She can taste the spiciness of the bourbon mixed with the effervescence of the champagne, and it's a delicious combination. Charley can feel the effects of the champagne taking over already, and she knows she needs to slow down, or she won't have a hope in hell of making it through the night.

She watches as more and more people come into the club, and she begins to wonder exactly what kind of club this is. The women are dressed very provocatively, and the men look beautifully polished. Charley is beginning to feel very out of place in her tailored jacket and skinny jeans.

Charley watches an interaction take place between Katherine and Peter. Katherine appears frazzled and angry. Peter looks calm and collected. Jeff tries hard to engage Charley in a conversation, but she is too interested in what is going on between Peter and Katherine. She begins to eavesdrop as much as she can, overhearing things from Peter like "you need to remember the rules" and "Jeff will be good, too." She catches the part of Katherine's sentence where she says,

"But it's not fair, I've been looking forward to all of us together since we decided to come here." Charley's ears perk up as she catches a tiny fragment of Peter's sentence. "Need her to myself ... break her in." Charley has no idea what is going on between them, but she is beginning to feel a little uncomfortable as she hears snippets of their conversation. She takes in the erotic art on the walls and then it begins to register that there are quite a few people who are kissing passionately and dancing suggestively, which adds to her unease. As Charley's brain tries to process what is going on, Katherine leaves her stool, excusing herself to the restroom.

Noticing that Charley's drink is low, Peter reaches across her to refill it. She stills his hand as she warns him, "I need to take it very easy, or I won't make it through the night."

Peter stops in mid-reach, leveling his face with hers and leans in for a kiss. It's not just any kiss. It's a kiss filled with passion and promise of things to come. Charley can feel the heat emanating from Peter's chest as he pulls her to her feet to deepen the kiss. Katherine's voice breaks through to Charley, ending their kiss as she proclaims, "I see it's time to get our party started."

Charley's thoughts are scattered as she begins to panic, wondering how she is going to deal with this.

Peter keeps his voice soft and smooth, "Ah yes, Katherine, I'm glad you have pulled yourself out of your funk and are ready to party. I believe it's time for you and Jeff to get to know each other better, so Charley and I can do the same."

As the seconds tick by, Charley's confusion and anxiety mount exponentially. Charley looks from Peter's face, to Katherine's, to Jeff's, hoping to find an answer. Finally, Charley can keep quiet no longer and begins to pepper all three of them with questions but fears the answers. She is not sure she can handle whatever it is they may tell her.

"What the hell kind of place is this? Why did we have to bring our own booze into a club? What conversations are you two having about me?" Looking around, Charley sees the activity level in the room has picked up. There are naked people licking, kissing, groping, and fondling each other. She looks to her left and sees a couple naked and writhing together on one of the couches.

"What the fuck is going on here?" Charley demands forcefully. Peter tries to quiet her. Her eyes blaze with burning anger. He explains smoothly, "Ah Bella, I've never been here before either, so I'm just as shocked as you are. Katherine and I just wanted to go someplace different and unique—you know, a place that's kind of off the beaten path a little, a place where we could be anonymous and have a little fun. I didn't expect to see people screwing on couches. All I expected were some deep, passionate kisses to tide us over until later."

The wind is knocked out of Charley's sails. She wants to believe what Peter is telling her. He actually appears sincere as he delivers his speech. He seems embarrassed and ashamed, and Charley can't help but feel a twinge of pity for him. He brought two women here without knowing what this place really was.

She looks around and takes a deep breath, realizing she is somewhat mollified but disgusted at the same time. This place is beyond anything she has ever experienced, but she doesn't see a way out. Katherine quietly slips away as Charley rants, and Peter tries to soothe her. She needs to make sure she is on top of her game now so she can stay out of trouble. She doesn't want to end up like these people in front of her—the ones who are panting, groaning, and doing unimaginable things in front of everyone. Peter whispers in her ear that he is going to find Katherine, so they can pack up and leave. Charley can't seem to take her eyes off what is happening around her. Nobody has any inhibitions. They don't care who watches as they go on doing all sorts of acts Charley couldn't have dreamed up if she hadn't seen them for herself.

Charley sits down on her stool to regain her equilibrium. Her purse is on the seat behind her, and she can feel a slight vibration coming from it. She opens it, almost expecting to find whatever Peter bought at the sex shop tucked inside. It is with a sense of relief, followed by a sense of foreboding that she sees it's her cell phone vibrating with a text message.

9:45 p.m.
Hey Char. I'm so sorry for the way I treated you when you left for New Orleans. You didn't deserve that. You wanted to go and have a good time— I wanted you to go and have a good time. You didn't need me piling my

shittiness on you. I'm sorry I made you jump through hoops. I hope the rest of your weekend is great. I loved seeing how happy you've been these past couple of weeks getting ready for this trip. You've been so excited, and I tried to ruin it for you. I miss you! But I want you to have fun, AND I called my mom and took the twins to the dentist ... they each got a clean bill of health. I know I don't tell you enough, but I love you ... always.

The color drains from Charley's face as she reads Garrett's text. Her mouth is still burning with Peter's kiss, and here she is reading loving words her husband has written to her. Remorse, shame, and guilt take over, as her brain goes into overdrive.

"Holy shit!" Charley exclaims, feeling the floor drop out from beneath her feet. "I need the bathroom. Where is it?" she asks one of the staff members. She is pointed in the right direction and heads to find it.

She comes across more rooms filled with people who are carnally exploring each other as she wends her way through the throng of people.

As she approaches the bathroom, she hears Katherine's voice saying, "See, I told you she couldn't handle this. You never should have brought her here. We should have gone back to the hotel, just the three of us. We could have worked our magic on her there."

Charley can hear Peter agreeing with Katherine. "I know we were taking a risk by bringing her here, but I still think it might work. I'll slip her a little something in her second drink to help calm her nerves. You know how much that pill helps everyone relax and get into what we're doing. I *need* to bring her into my collection. I can see behind the mask of naïveté she hides behind that she actually craves this kind of life. She just doesn't know it yet, but when she's in the collection, she'll realize how good this feels."

"Correction," Katherine snaps. "*Our* collection. Don't you forget that I've helped you get almost all of these women into your bed and onto your computer screen. They are ours. Those pictures are ours, and if you want Charley in our collection, you better figure out a way to get pictures of her so you can lock her in. Nobody leaves once we have our pictures. That is the only way you'll make sure Charley stays. She can't leave as long as you have that threat of exposure hanging over her head."

Charley can hear Katherine's voice continue, becoming low and seductive, "But now, you seem to have a problem ... now you have a rock-hard dick, and only one person to soothe it for you, baby. I know you have that private room reserved." Katherine practically purrs as she finishes with, "Why don't we take advantage of it? We can try out the toy you bought at the sex shop. I can tell you if I think Charley will like that particular clit clip or if you should find one like you bought me for our first time. Remember that? Let's relive that night. Charley will be fine for a few minutes. Your friend, Jeff, is with her. We can tell her I was so upset by what's happening in this place, and you needed to comfort me."

Overhearing their conversation answers all of Charley's questions. She turns around, quickly leaving the club and the craziness of Peter's strange world behind.

CHAPTER NINE

CHARLEY KNOWS the hotel is not far from where she is, and she needs the walk to clear her mind. She has so much to think about and process. She realizes, though, she must get back quickly so she can escape before Peter and Katherine figure out she's gone. She can only hope that they take their time doing whatever they're going to do in Peter's private room.

Luckily, Charley finds a cab to take her back to the hotel, and ride is quick. She overpays the cabbie as she rushes inside and upstairs to the room she shared with Katherine for the afternoon.

Her guilt is overwhelming. Charley can only hope that she can repair her marriage and if she can't, she has no one to blame but herself. She needs to catch the first plane home. Formulating a plan, she throws her suitcase back together. Charley figures she can get to the airport without anyone suspecting she left the hotel because it's so late.

Charley's bag is packed, and she is out the door heading down to the lobby, praying not to run into Peter and Katherine. Her heart is hammering in her chest as the elevator doors open. Rushing from the elevator, she bolts to the bellman's stand, asking for a cab. The bellman takes her request as well as her bag, as she tells him she'll be waiting in the bar.

Walking toward the bar, Charley hears her name being called. *Shit! I don't want to face anyone right now.*

She turns around slowly to find David and Kristy coming in from their evening. Seeing her face devoid of color and panic in her eyes, they ask in unison, "*What* happened to you?"

Charley is having a hard time holding herself together after the way the beginning of the evening played out and her near collapse into a world of adultery. Tears spill out of her eyes and onto her cheeks as she tries to gulp back a sob, "I really screwed up. I may have destroyed my marriage all because of my stupidity."

David's one-word response is "Peter." It was all he needed to say for Charley's story to come tumbling out.

David takes Charley by surprise when he continues, "I'm sorry Peter got to you. How did he reel you in? Promises of gifts? Flattery? Telling you he'd take you on exotic trips?"

"What the hell do you mean?" Charley demands.

David explains, "Peter is a player. I've been around him a long time, and I've seen it all. He started this game in college when we were roommates where he tried to 'collect' as many girls as he could by finding out their weaknesses and preying on them. He's played it ever since, adding more and more women to his 'collection,' as he calls them. I figured you knew the game and that you were willingly his latest prey."

Charley's mouth goes dry as she tries to absorb the words David is saying to her. "Are you fucking kidding me? This is a *game* he plays with women? This is a *game* he played with me where I nearly threw away the life I had for a ... Ah, *shit*! 'The rules.' *Now* I get it! I am such a dumbass! If I had a gun right now ... " she spat as the bellman came in to tell her the cab is ready.

"Whoa, wait ... you're leaving?" Kristy asks.

"I'm on the first flight out of here. I can't stay in the room with Katherine. She and Peter are in on this together. I have to leave. I've got a shitload of work to do at home. I need to try and salvage my marriage. I just hope I have the strength to get through all of this with my husband," Charley tells them.

"We're going to ride with you," Kristy tells her, as David nods in agreement.

"You need a friend right now, and we're here for you. I should have taken you aside and told you after you and Kristy sat reading the tarot cards this afternoon," David says sheepishly. "I should have known you were in over your head."

Charley is grateful for their company as the three walk to the lobby together. She feels a small measure of comfort knowing they are there and will help to avert any potential for unpleasant surprises.

Piling into the back seat of the cab, Kristy takes the lead on the conversation.

"Look, Charley, I know you're feeling pretty lousy right now, and part of me wants to slap you upside the head and say 'You should feel shitty!' but the other part of me understands. Peter is a suave, handsome guy who knows how to flatter the ladies. He can make the most stoic woman smile and swoon. I've seen it dozens of times, in college and in New York. We live not far from him now, so I see how he operates. If you're the least bit lonely or sad, he somehow picks up on it and pounces. It was wrong of me not to tell you this afternoon. And I'm sorry you're going to be dealing with some pretty bad stuff when you get home."

"But ..." Kristy adds, wiping a stray tear from Charley's cheek, "you need to go back through what the tarot cards told you. You need to be strong, and you need to realize we all screw up. There is some pretty amazing stuff in those cards—insights I can see that relate to your life and what you just told us." Kristy breaks eye contact with Charley, looks at David, and says, "Do you mind if I tell her?"

"No, she needs to hear it," he replies.

"I asked David for a divorce four years ago because things were just ... oh, how do I say it? Things were crappy between us. I was working closely with a guy, and I started to have feelings for him. I thought it would be good and fun to try something new. David and I got married very young, and our spark was gone. So when I told David I wanted a divorce, his response was, 'Why? What did I do wrong?' It's not that he did anything wrong, it's that he couldn't do anything right, at least in my mind. The guy at work was trying to win me over. He was working hard, and he was hitting all the right buttons, the ones David used to hit. I nearly cheated, too, but I asked David for a divorce before I did anything. Things were very strained between us after that, and I prepared paperwork to dissolve twenty years of marriage. David came to me one day as I was going through our list of assets and asked, 'Can we just try, one more time? I want to make this work. But I'll sign the paperwork immediately if you do one thing for me.' "

Kristy's eyes were full of tears as she continued on with her story, " 'I want us to go on this marriage encounter,' David told me, 'It's an intense, week-long workshop aimed at repairing failing marriages. I have made all the arrangements; all you have to do is say yes.' What can I say? I looked down at the papers I was working on, separating all of our twenty years of life together, and something hit me. I needed to try this, to see if we could repair and rebuild."

Kristy looked at Charley and told her, "You need to try and make it work, one more time—for your kids, for yourself, and for your husband. I won't lie. That was the hardest week of my life, but it made me realize what is really important and that's living a life with love." Kristy pulled out her wallet, found what she was looking for, and handed Charley a business card with the information for the marriage encounter.

She made her promise to give it a try if Garrett would let her.

"The two times I've met Garrett, he seemed like a kind man. He sat with me at one of the reunions and melted my heart with the way he talked about you. Joy shined in his eyes when he said your name. Charley, honey, I hope you can make this work. I want it to work for you," Kristy told Charley as she held her hand with the card in it.

David leaned across Kristy to take Charley's hand in his as well and added, "Kristy's right. That week was the hardest week of my life, but it made us the couple we are today. Strong and united."

The cab was pulling to the curb in front of the airport. Tears were coursing down Charley's face. She stepped out, trying hard to hold it together when her two friends got out to hug her good-bye and wish her luck on this next part of the journey.

"Just know, Charley, I'm only a phone call away if you need someone to talk to," Kristy offered, as David helped her back into the cab.

Charley waved good-bye to them until the cab was out of sight and slowly made her way into the terminal to rebook her ticket home.

* * *

Charley is now booked on the 5:00 a.m. flight out of New Orleans and scheduled to arrive in Louisville at noon. A two-hour wait for the flight to board looms in front of her. The tears are still there; she can feel the tightness in her throat every time she thinks of a kiss or a touch or a phrase she was dumb enough to take from Peter. She realizes now she had been living in a world of make-believe for the past few weeks. It wasn't real. It was fiction. And now, she can only hope to repair her real life so she can live a good, decent, and honorable life again.

Charley pulls out her tarot card book and sits down to reexamine it like Kristy told her to. First, she looks at the card representing the past. *"The Four of Wands."* Reading voraciously through her tears, she tries to see what Kristy told her to look for. Her eyes stop on a sequence of sentences toward the end of a paragraph in the middle of the page.

"In this picture, there are people milling about the city walls. They are a reminder that joy and tragedy go hand in hand. You cannot have one without the other. When there is a tragedy, life will go on and will return to normal at some point. There should be no sense of entitlement to constant, joyous rapture."

Is this truly me? Did I feel entitled to "constant, joyous rapture?" And will life truly return to normal at some point for me, after this massive fuckup?

Charley ponders what she has read for a little longer before moving on to the Lovers card in the present position of her tarot card reading.

She looks at the card itself and sees, again, the ripe symbolism of the Lovers being portrayed as Adam and Eve. The tree of knowledge and the serpent are just behind Eve. Charley completely equates herself with Eve. She ate from the tree of knowledge and has now fallen from grace. She reads to see what she can glean from this, and her eyes become fixed on the sentences, which read, "Adam and Eve serve as the symbol for every couple. Every relationship begins pure. Sometimes one, or both, of the partners wavers or falters. And then, the best must be pulled from the relationship after the initial bliss is gone, so the relationship is made whole again."

For the first time since she realized what was going on, a little sliver of hope springs up in Charley's chest. She knows these are just tarot cards, but for some reason, they are giving her the faith she needs to get through the upcoming days and weeks.

Next is the card she pulled in the future position. The Five of Cups. She remembers from earlier, there is a lot of meaning given to this card about things not going well in a person's life. "That's an understatement," she blurts out loud. She goes on to read the entire section, focusing on the passage describing not only the card but, in Charley's mind, herself as well.

Charley reads a bit further, stopping at this sentence, her tears falling on the page as she reads.

"If this card is in the future position, care must be paid by the person receiving this card, for this card may be telling them to closely examine all of the things in their lives that would break their hearts if drastic changes occurred."

Closing her eyes, Charley lets her tears fall silently down her cheeks, absorbing what she has just read.

* * *

Charley lets the tears fall until she can cry no more. She is thankful the terminal is nearly empty at 2:30 in the morning, as this sadness is hers to deal with alone. Fighting back a fresh wave of grief, a new emotion starts to take over. Anger. Anger at Peter and Katherine for pulling her into their life of games. She is angry with herself as well, but she has time to handle that later. Now, she needs to deal with Peter and Katherine.

4:10 a.m.

You two lead pitiful lives full of darkness, deceit, and falsity—a web woven in fiction and virtual lies. The life I have lived for the past two weeks is not one I intend to ever experience again. In life, you have to choose between right and wrong, fiction and reality. I choose right. I choose reality. My life may not have been the "exciting" kind of life you think you have, but my existence, before I got involved with you, was good and honorable and decent and real. I have a lot of work to do to fix my reality, but my reality is worth 2,000 of your fictitious, dark, pitiful lives. Do not ever call or contact me again.

Charley hits send as the cabin doors close, and the flight attendants announce their departure.

* * *

Charley's mind is racing, and her body is exhausted. She knows she has a long hard day ahead of her, so as soon as she sits down, she closes her eyes and tries to sleep. Her sleep is fitful and restless. She gets a few minutes of rest before her plane touches down in Charlotte where she'll change planes. One more leg of this journey is all that stands before her and all hell breaking loose where she might lose everything she holds dear because of her stupidity.

Sleep calls her one more time as her last airplane ascends, taking her closer to home. She sleeps until the flight attendant's voice comes over the speakers telling them they are in their final approach to Louisville International Airport.

Trying to buy herself more time, Charley allows the other passengers to deplane before she does. Her mind is muddled from her extreme sleep deficit. Shaky from lack of food, her body revolts at the thought of eating anything to regain her strength. Standing up on wobbly legs, Charley gathers her suitcase and walks slowly down the jetway and into the airport. She feels like she has a giant scarlet "A" plastered on her chest. She senses everyone is staring at her, condemning all of the actions and misdeeds from the past weeks. Shame and sorrow threaten to swallow her.

Finally, Charley arrives at Christina's little bug, loads her suitcase in the trunk, and starts the car. With trembling hands, she puts the car in reverse and backs out of the parking spot. She begins to rehearse what she is going to say to Garrett, although she wonders how she is going to tell him what happened and why it happened. Charley has to figure out a way to focus the upcoming conversation on rebuilding their marriage. She knows now that Garrett loves her, and it may be too late. She only hopes she gets the chance to tell him how much she loves him, too.

Her eyes are heavy, and her hands are shaking harder and harder with each passing mile. Charley hears her phone ding with an incoming text. She reaches into her bag, glancing down for only a second to see that Garrett has texted her again.

She looks up; her eyes grow huge as she screams, "Oh, shit! No!"

CHAPTER TEN

GARRETT'S PHONE DINGS with a page. He looks down to see that a trauma patient is being transported in. His page reads, "Forty-two-year-old female. Involved in an MVA. Extrication time, 15 minutes. PT is unresponsive with facial trauma. Intubated at the scene. Fluids being delivered. ETA 10 min."

It's going to get busier now. He has also just gotten a page for two patients with gunshot wounds coming in on top of a motorcyclist who is already here. He calls his staff in and gives them the briefing.

"Forty-two-year-old female involved in a car accident is en route. ETA is ten minutes. She was unresponsive at the scene and is intubated. We also have two gunshot wounds coming in. ETA on them is twenty minutes."

The nursing staff and residents know what they are supposed to do. It's a well-run and extremely efficient ER. They are well prepared.

Their first patient arrives, and the residents get to work examining her. She has a bleeding head wound. Her right eye is swollen shut. Her lip is split open and bleeding. Dr. Ciucci, the chief resident, is examining her. She methodically makes her way through the patient's injuries, stopping at her chest and noting the extreme bruising of her ribs and the soft tissue of her belly. With the patient stabilized, Dr. Ciucci explains to Garrett that she is sending her patient for a full trauma scan. She explains about the extreme bruising on the ribs and abdomen. Garrett takes notes as she rattles off the injuries. He tells Dr. Ciucci to send the patient to get her CT scan and says, "OK, let's get prepared to welcome our gunshot wounds to our ER."

With that, the bay doors open to one of the gunshot victims. Garrett can hear him yelling loudly and demanding pain meds. The second gunshot victim is brought in, and he can be heard yelling at the first gunshot wound victim, "I can't wait to get out of here, so I can shoot your stupid ass again. And this time, I won't miss!" The police come in with these two. Both are shackled to their gurneys.

"Thankfully," Garrett can be heard saying. The yelling keeps escalating, but Garrett knows these two are receiving the best care possible, so there is no reason to get involved.

The motor vehicle accident victim is wheeled back into the ER with the diagnosis of pools of blood in her abdomen. "Take her to the OR, STAT, and get her prepped for surgery. I'm on my way now to scrub in. Dr. Ciucci, I want you in there with me," Garrett says to his chief resident.

Walking side by side, the two doctors go over the results from the trauma patient's CT scan. Based on the location of the blood, Garrett believes she has a lacerated liver. The pool of blood in her belly is growing bigger by the second, and he's anxious to get in there to fix her up. "She is somebody's wife, mother, sister, daughter," he says out loud. "It's time to go save her."

The doctors walk into the OR to find their patient ready to go. Her body is completely draped and prepped for surgery. Her hair has been tucked into a surgical bonnet, and she is fully sedated. It is time to begin. Garrett steps up to the table, picks up a scalpel, and prepares to make his incision when the top of a tattoo on her left side catches his eye. He's seen it somewhere before, but he can't quite remember where. He places the tip of the blade against her skin when it hits him. That's Charley's tattoo. God knows, he's seen it often enough. He's traced it with his fingers so many times, it's almost become a part of him. He puts his finger on the top edge of the wing of her tattoo, stopping dead in his tracks.

"What is this patient's name?" he calls out to the OR. They are all stunned. Never have they heard a doctor ask for the name of a patient in the middle of surgery.

His face turns ash white as one of the nurses reads the name on the clipboard, "*Oh fuck*, Dr. Dempsey. I think it's your wife. Her name is Charlene Dempsey."

Garrett nods once as his hands stay poised over Charley's abdomen. Dr. Ciucci asks if he'd like her to take over. He feels calmness spread through his body, as he says, "No, this is my wife ... I need to do this. I want to do this. I know you're here if I need you, Doctor, but Charley needs me."

Garrett makes his incision. He is quick to locate the laceration of her liver and deftly makes repairs. The bleeding is slowing down but hasn't stopped completely. Garrett keeps looking. He knows there has to be another laceration in there somewhere. He finds a second wound to her liver on posterior side and works quickly and efficiently, making precise sutures to finally stop the bleeding. His hands are steady, but his heartbeat is erratic as thoughts of losing Charley begin to hit him. After making sure all of the bleeding has stopped and that her internal wounds are completely stitched up, Garrett turns over the job of closing her up to Dr. Ciucci.

At that moment, a nurse steps into the OR and addresses him, "Dr. Dempsey, a couple of state troopers are here to see you. I told them you were in surgery, but they said it was urgent that they talk to you."

Garrett walks out of the OR knowing they are here to tell him about Charley's accident. He meets them in the hallway with his face ghostly white and tears threatening to spill.

With a trembling voice he says to them, "I know why you're here. I just finished surgery on my wife. She had massive internal injuries that I'm sure will heal, but I don't know about the head trauma she suffered. I haven't had a chance to see for myself how bad it is." Garrett knows these two fairly well.

They have delivered many patients to him over the years, and they have always been compassionate with the families when they have delivered bad news of any magnitude.

Trooper Scott Johnson is the first to speak. "I'm so sorry, Doc. We were the first ones on the scene, and the accident was nothing like I've ever seen. The car is nearly unrecognizable. She is lucky she didn't have a passenger with her. That person wouldn't have made it."

Garrett swallows a couple of times, trying to regain his composure at the thought of Charley being killed in a car accident. His words are low and filled with emotion as he manages to say, "Tell me what happened."

Trooper Kevin Miller spoke first, "She got tangled up with an eighteen-wheeler. According to witness accounts, she was in the left lane, preparing to pass when the driver of the semi started to drift into her lane and then jerked back, causing the trailer to slam into the car on the passenger side. Skid marks on the road indicate that she tried to stop but ended up going under the back end of the trailer, shearing off the left side of the car and wedging it under the truck. It took fifteen minutes to free her from the wreckage and get her to you."

"I don't understand how a Sequoia can get wedged under a semi. It doesn't make any sense," Garrett says, trying to comprehend the accident scene.

"Doc, she was in a little red bug. She wasn't in a Sequoia," Trooper Johnson told him.

And that's when it hits him. She's not supposed to be home yet. She's still supposed to be in New Orleans and headed to watch the NCAA basketball tournament today. Now that he is processing things, he remembers sending her a text telling her to have fun at the game today not long before he got the page about her coming in.

"She's not supposed to be home yet. Did she say anything to you?" Garrett asks the troopers.

"No. She was unresponsive when we arrived on the scene. We did get her purse and her phone out of her car though," Johnson tells Garrett, handing over a bag containing some of her belongings.

"We saw that there was a suitcase in the trunk, but we left it there. Here is where the car was towed. And here is the receipt for what was cataloged in the car. Again, Doc, I'm sorry about your wife, and I truly hope she's OK. Here's my card. Please call me if you need anything. I'll get this report written up, and then you can see it. Can we answer any more questions for you, Doc?" Johnson asks.

Garrett answers quietly, "No. Thank you both. You've been more than kind."

Both troopers give Garrett a quick squeeze on the shoulder and walk back to their waiting squad cars as Garrett walks to the post-anesthesia care unit to check on Charley. Her eye is completely swollen shut, and a massive wound has been bandaged just below her hairline. Her lips are bruised, battered, and swollen. He knows the swelling in her brain could be increasing, minute by minute, as he listens to the machine breathing for her. The doctor in him can't help but take over, checking the machines keeping track of her vital signs. They are stable, which is exactly what he wants to see. He stops his examination and looks at Charley, really looks at her. She seems so little and vulnerable lying on the gurney with all of the tubes sticking out. He hadn't realized how thin she'd gotten and stops to wonder why. Her arms are lying on top of the covers and they look small and frail. Her once-rosy cheeks are chalk white. Her dark, thick eyelashes are closed, barring him from seeing her beautiful blue eyes. He hangs his head as tears slip down his cheeks.

"Please don't die, Charley," he begs, grasping her hand.

The nurses come in to find Garrett standing beside his wife, grief-stricken. Telling gently him it's time to move her to the ICU, they begin to roll the bed with Garrett walking slowly beside them. He can't seem to find the courage to release her hand as they make their way, carefully, to her room.

Garrett sits down in a chair as Charley is settled in. He realizes he is still carrying her purse and knows it is time to try and figure out why she is here at the hospital and not in New Orleans. He starts with the one person who might know. He calls Gayle. His voice is thick with emotion as she answers the phone.

"Gayle, it's Garrett. I'm on Charley's phone. She's been in a massive accident and is here at the hospital with me," he says to her.

"I'm on my way, Garrett." He can hear the panic rising in her voice. "No! Wait. What? You just said she's at the hospital with you. Are you in New Orleans?"

"No, Charley's here at U of L with me. That's part of the reason I'm calling you. Did you know she was coming home?"

"No. I had no idea she was planning to come home early. I haven't talked to her since she left. I was letting her have fun with her classmates, so I left her alone. Garrett, I'm on my way, but please tell me, is she going to be OK?" Gayle asks, quietly.

"Gayle, at this point, I don't know. Her body has been through a lot today. Just come down. I'll fill you in when you get here, and maybe together, we can figure out why she's home early."

* * *

Gayle wastes no time arriving at the hospital. She left the kids in the care of a neighborhood babysitter and raced to the hospital. Garrett had texted her Charley's room number, and she somberly walks in to find Garrett sitting by Charley's bed with his head bent over her, holding her hand. Gayle comes up quietly beside him, lays her hand on his shoulder and says nothing. She gasps as her eyes take in all of the tubes and machines keeping Charley alive. Charley's head is heavily bandaged, but Gayle can see her beautiful face has been bashed and damaged. She takes her hand from Garrett's shoulder and begins to caress Charley's face.

"Oh, Garrett! She looks so much worse than I envisioned. What happened?"

Garrett fills Gayle in with what the state troopers told him, and her blood runs cold at the thought of Charley being in such a massive accident. She hugs herself as Garrett explains all of Charley's injuries. Garrett tells Gayle he hasn't even begun to think about Charley's prognosis. He goes on to say that he can't begin to imagine anything except for the best outcome.

The two sit together, listening to the buzzing, whirring, and beating of the machines when Garrett finally manages to ask, "Why did she come home? If she were still in New Orleans, she wouldn't be here right now."

Gayle reaches out her hand to him and just holds on tight. She is the first one to think of looking through Charley's purse for an answer. Picking it up, Gayle begins to search the contents.

She pulls out the book on tarot cards and gives a small laugh. "It's just like Charley to try out the voodoo places." Gayle opens the book to the page where all of the tarot cards are tucked, and as she is looking through them, she finds the business card for the marriage encounter workshop. *That's odd,* she thinks to herself but is hoping that maybe she is thinking of asking Garrett to go with her. While Gayle is looking through the book, Garrett starts to scroll through her phone looking for answers. Out of the corner of her eye, she sees him stop cold.

"Gayle, what's this?" Garrett demands, with a hard edge to his voice. "There better be some damn good explanation for this. Who the hell are Peter and Katherine? And what are they doing with *my* wife?"

Gayle looks up to see Garrett standing over her with Charley's phone in his hands.

Gayle tentatively takes the phone from Garrett's hands and begins to read. Her face drains of all color as she finishes. "Fuck! What did she do?"

Garrett voice is cold as ice, "Did you know about whatever this is?" He takes the phone from her, looking back through her texts with Peter.

"I didn't know I was going to be played for a fool when I said Charley could go on her little trip," he says with a steel glint in his eye.

"Listen, you and I don't know what happened down there. I do know I told Charley to be careful of that guy she was texting. From what little she told me, he seemed way too interested in her. But from what I see on the text, Charley told them to piss off." Gayle takes a calming breath and continues, "Like I said, I don't know what happened in New Orleans, but here's what I do know about Charley and her mind-set before she left."

Gayle proceeds to tell Garrett about her lunch conversation with Charley, sparing no details, from Charley's extreme sadness to the nastiness his mother has inflicted on her through the years. Gayle finishes her tale by telling Garrett that answers to a lot of this can probably be found in Charley's journals.

"Journals? What journals?" Garrett asks, allowing a deadly calm to permeate his own mind-set.

He's beyond stunned to think that Charley would go off on a trip to hook up with another man. Looking through the texts, he can't understand how she could believe what this shithead was writing to her. He feels a red-hot rage burning just beneath the surface.

"How do you *not* know about her journals? She's been keeping them since before I met her. She has one for each year and she keeps them all in chronological order in her office," Gayle continues. "Listen, Garrett. Charley needs—" The blaring of one of Charley's machines cuts off Gayle. Three nurses come running in, knowing it's Dr. Dempsey's wife who's in distress.

The anger that Garrett feels toward Charley is automatically switched to concern for his patient. He tries to forget about what she may have done in New Orleans. Garrett's transformation from angry husband to caring doctor happens before in one of Charley's heartbeats, and Gayle's admiration for Garrett grows exponentially as she stands in the background, with tears staining her cheeks, hoping and praying her best friend will pull through. Garrett slumps over Charley as the latest crisis seems to be averted for the moment, and he turns his attention back to Gayle.

"All right, Gayle, what does Charley need?"

"You. She needs you. Don't give up on her now. See what she has to say in her journals and then see what she has to say when she wakes up." Her voice catches on the word *when*.

Garrett knows she's right, but his anger at the thought of being made a fool of is getting the better of him. He knows he needs to calm down and think about all of this before Charley wakes up.

"Can you stay with her while I go home, tell the kids, and try to find some answers?" Garrett asks. "I don't want her alone if she wakes up."

"Of course, I can stay," Gayle reassures him. "Jack should be home soon, so the boys are taken care of."

"I have to go by and pick up my boys. I need all of the kids there at the same time to tell them what has happened to their mom."

Gayle nods in agreement, and then as a last minute thought, pushes the book of tarot cards into his hands. She doesn't know why she thinks he needs them, but something tells her Charley would want him to see whatever it was she had underlined in there.

* * *

Garrett drives straight to Gayle's house and runs to the front door to pick up his boys. He quickly loads them in the car and then puts calls in to Christina and Noelle letting them know he is on his way home with news. The boys are quiet on the ride home, as if they know and understand that something has happened but are too afraid to ask what it is. Garrett gets home just as Christina is pulling the Sequoia in the driveway with her two younger sisters, and his heart gives a little lurch wondering if Charley's accident would have been less severe if she had been driving her car. He vows to go out and get Christina an SUV as soon as Charley is stabilized.

Garrett leads them all into the kitchen and whips up a batch of hot cocoa as he speaks, hoping the special brew Charley always makes for them will help soften the blow of knowing their mom is in an intensive care bed in the hospital. They all take it like he thought they would. Shock settles into fear as they circle around him looking for the love and support their mom always gives them. He hugs each one tightly, offering comfort in this time of instability. The questions are coming fast and furious. Garrett is trying his best to answer honestly, but he is also trying to shield his kids a little from the harsh reality of their mom's condition. The questions finally stop as Garrett and his children sit together in their big kitchen that lacks cheer without Charley.

Charley's phone rings as they sit drinking their cocoa. It is a number Garrett doesn't recognize, but he knows he needs to answer it. "Hello, this is Charley's phone. How can I help you?" Garrett asks in a flat voice wondering if the caller is Peter.

"Oh, hi, this is Kristy. I'm a friend of Charley's from high school. Is this Garrett?"

"Yes, this is Garrett. How can I help you, Kristy?" comes Garrett's cold reply. He doesn't know which, if any, of her high school friends, he can trust.

"Hi, Garrett. You and I have met a couple of times at our reunions. I was just telling Charley how highly I thought of you when you stayed and chatted with me. You said the sweetest things about her, and I really enjoyed talking to you. It was so good to learn Charley married such a great guy," the words come rushing out of her mouth.

"I'm sorry I'm rambling. I wasn't expecting you to answer her phone, but I'm glad I caught you. I'd like to chat with you again in a little bit. Right now, though, I was hoping to catch Charley. I just wanted to check up on her. Is she around?" Garrett hears her nerves through the phone line.

Garrett's tone softens a little as her words sink in. He feels, somehow, she wasn't a part of what happened in New Orleans. He also knows she might know something that might be of help to him.

"No, Kristy," he says more softly than minutes before, "she is not here. She's in a coma in the hospital. She had a massive car accident on the way home from the airport."

Garrett can hear her sharp intake of air as she says, "Oh my, God! No! Please tell me she's going to be OK!'

"At this point, we don't know an exact prognosis. It's too early," Garrett replies, going on to explain the situation.

"As far as I'm concerned, there is no reason to pretend with you about what I know. You're a smart guy, and I can only assume you know something went wrong in New Orleans." Her reply doesn't come as a shock to Garrett. Her response lets him know he will get some answers.

"She was so sad and so scared when my husband and I left her at the airport. Her heart was breaking, and she was so mad at herself for letting Peter into her life."

From there, the entire story comes tumbling out. Garrett listens in stunned silence to the sordid tale of what happened in New Orleans and how Charley left as soon as she figured out what was going on.

Kristy goes on to tell him the same story she told Charley in the cab ride over. She finishes by trying to reassure him, "Charley knows she screwed up. She left Peter when she realized where things were going. Her regret and remorse were stronger than anything I've ever felt. She hoped you would be able to forgive her. I hope you can, too. Everyone deserves a second chance. You guys especially deserve it. You were such a sweet couple to watch. There is something special about you two. I could see it at the reunions. I hope you can find it again."

Garrett doesn't know what to say, but he realizes there is a lot of work to do for them to be together again. *If Charley survives,* a little voice in the back of his head says.

He ends the conversation by thanking Kristy for being so honest and promising to keep her updated on Charley.

He then goes to Charley's office, turns on the light, and begins to look for her journals.

* * *

Garrett finds them just as Gayle said he would, chronologically arranged within her bookshelves. He works from the present one back in time until he gets to the year they met. Seventeen journals in all are loaded into a shopping bag, ready to be transported to the hospital. He goes downstairs to tell the kids he is headed back to the hospital and is met with pleas to come with him. They all want to see their mom. He knows it's useless to say no, but he also knows he is staying the night. He calls Gayle to see if she can bring the kids home as he hears Christina behind him offering to drive them home. Part of him wants to let Christina bring them back, but the other part of him is shaken to the core, knowing his wife is in intensive care because of a traffic accident. She's an experienced driver, and she nearly lost her life behind the wheel of a car.

He excuses himself from Gayle as she tells him she can bring the kids home. He turns to Christina, "Honey, I know you can drive home, but it's been a rough day for me. I would feel so much better if Gayle would drive you all back to the house from downtown. It can get a little confusing down there, and I would never forgive myself if anything happened to you all. So please don't argue with me, just let Gayle drive you."

Christina acquiesces, walks over to hug him and quietly says, "Thanks, Dad. I didn't really want to drive. Right now, I don't want to be behind the wheel of the car."

Garrett and the kids arrive at the hospital to find Gayle in the seat next to the bed and Charley exactly as he had left her — machines working to keep her alive. Gayle gets up, scoops the kids tightly into her arms and cries with them as they each realize the magnitude of their mom's condition. The fear in the room is palpable — each person's worry compounding on another's. Garrett tries hard to keep everyone calm, but he knows that Charley's prognosis is tenuous at this point. They will have a better idea of where she is after twenty-four hours.

As the children gather around their mom, Peter pulls Gayle off to the side and tells her about Kristy's call. He shows her the journals he has brought with him, telling Gayle he will read them so he can understand what is going on. He stops his conversation with Gayle when he hears Amanda crying and Andrew trying hard to soothe her. Andrew is the one who always tries to console and make things better for others. He would give you the shirt off his back, and he wears his heart on his sleeve.

Garrett looks down at his twelve-year-old son with a sense of pride and déjà vu. It is almost like he is looking at a masculine version of Charley. His mind wanders to thoughts of who his wife really is.

She, like Andrew, wears her heart on her sleeve. Joy, passion, love and sorrow flit easily across her expressive face. Anyone who asks for her love is given it, without reservations and without strings attached. Sometimes, she gives it to the wrong people, but that never stops her from giving affection to others. She is the heart and soul of this family, and it hits Garrett hard, realizing how little he's been there for her recently. He needs to read her journals so that when—not if—she wakes up, he can understand where they are now and where their future may lead. As anxious as he is to read, though, he knows he needs to stay right here with his kids for now. They need him, and Charley needs them.

* * *

Garrett lets the kids stay until he sees Amanda's head droop against Charley's arm. She has fallen asleep. He knows they are exhausted and need to go home to rest. It could be a long road for them. He leans over to Gayle and whispers, "Can you take them home, please?" He doesn't want to upset them, but he knows they have had enough. And there is nothing more for them here tonight.

"Do you want them to come to my house, or would it be better if I just stay at your house with them?" Gayle asks.

"I would really appreciate it if you could stay with them at our house, so they have a little sense of the familiar. But I can always call my mom to come over and stay with them," Garrett offers.

"No. Please let me stay with them. I need to have them near me," Gayle replies immediately.

Gayle and Garrett get to work prying the kids out of Charley's room. He hugs each of them to him with a ferocity he didn't know he had. He realizes now he has spent many years taking his family for granted. With the kids gone and the room quiet, Garrett sits down to read Charley's journals to figure out what went wrong.

Garrett digs through the bag to find the journal from when they met almost seventeen years ago. It's almost as if he can hear Charley telling him where to look. He feels her heartbeat against his hand, and in the steady beat beneath his fingers, he can feel her voice in his head. Not only is she telling him how to look for answers, he can feel her asking for help. He is taken aback at the unbidden thoughts coming into his head. He hasn't heard her ask for help in so long ... why now?

"Why not now?" he imagines her saying. "Please read," he hears. He desperately wants those words to come from Charley's lips, so he does what he imagines her asking him to do. He reads. Garrett reads through the night, stopping here and there to absorb what Charley has had to say all of these years. His first look into the workings of his wife's mind is the year they first met. He lets himself go back to the first time he laid eyes on the most beautiful woman he had ever seen ...

I have to say I just found a guy I can't believe existed. He's beautiful and charming, and can I just say "WOW!" I hope to see him again soon!!

Let me set the stage...

I was scheduled on a flight to Hawaii. I showed up at the appointed time, met up with my coworkers on the flight. I was given my zone assignment, which wasn't my favorite part of the plane to work. I was given business class, and usually on these long flights to Hawaii, some businessmen get a little rowdy. These passengers are headed out for a conference or an incentive trip, so they can get a bit noisy and, well, obnoxious. I wasn't looking forward to it, but I knew there wasn't much use in complaining. I've worked with the crew leaders before, and it's not worth throwing a fit over. They get their feathers ruffled too easily, so I just mentally prepared myself and began to get situated. I stowed my bag and got to work.

I heard a group of guys board the plane. It was just as I expected. They had already been to the bar and were raring to continue their path to complete inebriation on the five-hour flight to LAX. I steeled my nerves and kept my head down with my poker face affixed.

We got everyone boarded, seated, and comfortable. As the plane taxied down the runway, I could hear these guys cracking up at what I guessed was some inane joke. Great, just great. This should be a blast, I thought.

Finally, we leveled off enough, and it was time to get to work. I was thankful I had Sarah with me as my "wingman." She and I can speak volumes about people just by a glance over the cart. I knew we would have a blast talking about these bozos after we were finished. What I didn't know was that I was going to be greeted by the prettiest, sparkliest green eyes I have ever seen. I guess they can't quite qualify as totally green, as there were hints of gold flecks in them, too. I guess that's what made them so stinking sparkly. God, they were gorgeous ... the only problem was that he was sitting with the bozos I couldn't wait to make fun of.

While the rest of the guys made sure to be as loud and obnoxious as they could, acting like idiots at a frat party, "Green Eyes" just smiled politely as he asked me for a Bloody Mary. I've had enough experience with drunks to know that he'd had a couple of drinks, but at least he wasn't as horrible and obnoxious as the guys sitting next to him. His friends were all busy trying to one-up each other and get our attention, but he was different. Not shy, just sweet. He asked about my day—how I liked flying for a living, where I lived. Nice conversational things ... not obnoxious comments like, "What's your room number? We'll come up and show you all how to party!"—which is what all of his friends were doing.

His friends finally passed out, with an hour and half to go. Finally. I had long since put my cart away and was kind of in "chill" mode when he made his way to the galley, asking for some water. He stayed and chatted with me, about what, I really don't remember. I just recall feeling so comfortable talking to him. As jerky as his friends were, he was the opposite.

He finally introduced himself to me. His name is Garrett Dempsey, and he made my heart flutter just a little with his deep voice and soft eyes.

He stayed in the galley for quite some time, continuing our conversation. He asked where I was staying when I got to Hawaii. Usually, it's just a quick layover hotel and then back on the plane, but for once, I took some time off on the back end of the trip. I made this work trip into a vacation, too, and I decided to splurge a little. OK, I actually splurged a lot, but it was my graduation present from my parents, and I had been saving up for just this kind of trip. I wanted to make my vacation something memorable, so I decided the best thing to do was take a quick island hop and head to Maui. I love Maui, and to sweeten the prospect of a Hawaiian vacation, I was staying at the Ritz. I got such a fabulous deal, I couldn't pass it up. Gayle was going to meet me there in a couple of days, meaning I was going to be solo initially. I felt my excitement about my trip come out as a gush ... I hoped I didn't turn him off with all of my excitement. But I don't think I did because he went on to tell me that's exactly where he was staying, too. And for some reason, it didn't shock me a bit that he was staying there—maybe divine providence. Who knows? In my head, I did a little happy dance. I was looking forward to maybe, just maybe, being able to get to know him better.

For the remainder of the trip, I was kept busy, busy, busy. There was not much time for idle chitchat, as one woman had a mild anxiety attack, and one of Garrett's friends woke up a little on the sick side after indulging himself just a bit too much. There was a fussy baby, a man who thought he was having a heart attack, and another woman who decided to argue with the passenger sitting next to her. And this wasn't even the craziest flight I'd ever been on.

We cleaned up the plane during the layover at LAX. Everyone re-boarded, including Garrett and settled in for the six-hour flight to Honolulu. The flight was like clockwork, and I did get to spend a little more time with Garrett, but not too much. I didn't want to come on too strong or seem desperate, so I tried hard to play it cool. It's such a fine line to walk ... not coming off desperate but wanting to seem interested, at the same time. It's made even harder in the close confines of a 767.

When we landed in Honolulu, Garrett shook my hand and said he truly hoped to see me at the Ritz while I was vacationing. My hand seemed to tingle from where he touched it ... sounds goofy I know, but it just felt so stinking good to shake his hand. They were warm and soft without a hint of a callous. I loved the feel of his hand holding mine ... again, goofy but I couldn't help it. I got to work straightening up the aircraft so I could continue on my merry way to my much-needed vacation.

Garrett and his friends were long gone by the time I was finished and ready to go. I caught my connecting flight, got a cab, and made it to the hotel ready for time in the sun. The hotel staff got me settled into my room nicely. I threw on my bikini and headed down to the pool. I heard them before I saw them. The drunks from the plane remained on their same path. I don't know how they kept going as long as they have, but they were in full-on party mode.

I quietly made my way to a lounge chair by the pool, put my hat on, grabbed my book, and settled in to read ... OK, really I was scanning the pool deck for Garrett, but I didn't want him to know that. A pool-side server showed up at my chair with a drink in his hand and said, "This is courtesy of that gentleman over there." He pointed to a guy sitting in a lounge chair *near where the rowdy group from the plane sat. The blonde hair gave him away. Garrett bought me a drink. I lifted my cocktail to him as he did the same, and we toasted across the pool.*

I played it cool and stayed where I was, hoping he would, at some point, come and sit with me for a bit. I got so involved in reading Midnight in the Garden of Good and Evil that I didn't hear him approach with a fresh cocktail. He complimented me on my choice of reading material as he sat down beside me and offered me the drink. I have to say, I was bit surprised he left his rowdy boys to come over, but I thoroughly enjoyed his company.

Garrett came back to the present and looked at his wife in the hospital bed, desperately wanting to see the happy vibrant girl he met in 1996 and not the battered and bruised Charley who was fighting for her life. To keep his mind from focusing on the worst, he continued reading a little more from her journal and their first meeting.

Good God, is there anything worse than having the "pleasure" of watching men try to pick up women? What a comedy scene and, to some degree, a complete and utter tragedy. I stood at the bar tonight and watched Garrett's friends trying to hit on every woman who walked near them. Men make me laugh out loud with their dimwitted pick-up lines. Do they seriously not know what it takes to win a woman over? I know women recognize what they want, so I'll write it down here, in black and white ... sort of a list of rules.

I remember the book from a few years ago about rules women need to follow to land the man of their dreams. Well, I'm thinking men need to follow a few, too. The dating scene is a game. Here's what I'd like to tell these guys, so they know how to win the game and the girl. I know guys like to compete and win, so why not give them some pointers to help them get there? Not that they'd ever follow these rules, but a girl can hope, can't she?

1. Be sincere. Women like sincerity. Women like to feel just a little special in the eyes of a guy. Little compliments here and there ... something, anything, to make a woman feel just a tiny bit more special than she did a minute before. Pretty eyes, beautiful smile ... anything from the neck up. No boobs, no butts, no curves, just something sincere about who she is as person not as an object.

2. Most women cringe when they hear a cheesy pick-up line. Really, they do. So don't do it.

3. DO NOT, and I repeat, DO NOT tell a woman you just met what you want to do to her. Telling her you want to "lick her" will either result in a swift kick to the groin or uncontrollable laughter at your ineptitude and sheer idiocy ... or maybe a combination of both. And yes, a guy from tonight actually told me he'd like to lick me "there"... where "there" refers to is anyone's guess since I turned on my heels and walked away before I could deliver said kick to groin.

4. Conversation is the key to being connected to a woman. Women need to feel emotionally connected, and they get there through conversation. Without conversation, there is no connection. Without a connection there is nothing. So, talk and listen, and talk some more. Believe me, it will make, and keep, the connection. For men, the key to connection is physical, but without an emotional connection, the physical connection fizzles.

5. Don't come on so strong. Be soft and gentle. This one could also be called "Back off, Bozo"! Do men REALLY think we want to be pawed and groped? Refer to above rule!!!
CONVERSATION!

6. Most women like a little romance. Just a little. It doesn't have to be a full-blown, major affair. Just a tiny, little show of something to let her know she's on your mind.

What little thing does she just love? Starbucks, Diet Coke, a flower? Surprise her with her favorite little something.

7. Respect. Women like to be and feel respected. Aretha Franklin had it right. R-E-S-P-E-C-T.

There are more, I am sure, but I want to keep it simple. From my experience, men need simple rules. From what I know about guys, they are, as a whole, not that deep. So the simpler I keep it, the better off men will be.

For the first time since he saw Charley's tattoo in the OR, Garrett laughed out loud. He had forgotten about the bar scene with the guys that night. He remembered watching Charley as she shook her head at his friends. Now he knows why. He turns the page and finds Charley's list of "rules" for the ladies.

MY RULES
OK, so yesterday, I wrote some rules for men. Today, I'm going to throw a few out there for the ladies. Like I wrote yesterday, love is a game, and I've decided games should have rules.

For the ladies:

1. *Be a little less available.* Back off just a little—you could also think of it as "stop smothering." Guys, even married guys, like the thrill of the chase.

2. *Be active.* Find some activities that interest you and keep you occupied in a good way. This goes back to the above rule. If you have some of your own activities, you won't be all up in your guy's grill.

3. *Be quiet.* If you volunteer to watch a game with your guy watch it ... quietly. Don't bitch, don't whine, don't complain, and don't talk too much. (I fail at the last one, sometimes.) A thought or question pops into my head every now and again, and it shoots out of my mouth before I know it, but mostly, if I'm watching a game with guys, my questions are about the game on TV.

4. *Be yourself.* I think the absolute worst advice any woman (or man, for that matter) can get is to change who they are for someone else. (I hate Cosmo's advice to women on what they need to change to get a guy ... REALLY, if you have to change who you are, it's NOT you!) Trying to live up to someone else's expectations of you is exhausting. I know, I've done it—many times. And it sucks! You can't keep up a charade in life. It doesn't work, so why Cosmo thinks it's a good idea for us to change to please a guy is beyond me.

5. *Be self-confident.* It's totally sexy—for both genders—to have self-confidence. But women tend to lack it a little too much sometimes, and men seem to have an overabundance when they should tone it down a notch or two. When women are confident, we strut our stuff with amazing grace. I don't think being self-confident means being perfect ... in fact, it's just the opposite. Being perfect is too much pressure, and our confidence can fly right out the door. Being self-confident is being happy in your own skin. It's a tough battle for women, but it's worth it, and it's totally, one hundred percent cool!

6. *Be respectful.* I will say it again ... Aretha Franklin had it right "R-E-S-P-E-C-T!" Respect yourself and your love, always.

7. *Be kind.* Sometimes we treat strangers much better than we treat the ones we love. Remember to say please and thank you, always. It goes a LONG way!

Garrett's heart constricts a little thinking about these rules and how Charley seemed to apply some to herself, but not all. When they first met, she was the most self-confident, sexy woman he had ever met. She had her choice of guys, and she chose him. He couldn't believe his luck. He remembers thinking and admiring her for always being herself and never bending to the will of the group. If she wanted to do something, she'd do it. She knew when she didn't want to do something, and she never wavered from her convictions. He didn't understand why she had lost that self-confidence he so fell in love with.

Garrett pages ahead in her journal. He wants to see what she thought about his proposal being followed so quickly by her pregnancy with Christina.

Garrett proposed! Down on one knee, knight-in-shining-armor kind of proposal. Tonight was our six-month anniversary since we met on the flight to Hawaii. He made reservations for us at Ruth's Chris, and off we went. Dinner was fabulous, of course (it is Ruth's Chris, for goodness' sake)! The steaks were unbelievable. Dessert couldn't have been topped, though! He had the entire wait staff in on his secret. His grin was broad and devilish, but a little shy at the same time. His hands were shaking as the wait staff came bearing two chocolate sin cakes with a card attached to one. They surrounded our table as our waiter gave me the card that read:

"Charley, here's a little bit of sin on a plate.
But life for me has been heaven since our very first date.
Will you do me the honor of my life?
And say yes to becoming my wife?"

I looked up to see Garrett staring at me with that melt-me-all-over look, as he got down on one knee and the wait staff asked, "Will you marry him?" What could I say, but YES?? He put the most gorgeous ring on my finger, and the entire restaurant erupted in applause as he swept me out of my chair and kissed me like I've never been kissed before ... a toe-curling, spine-tingling, hair-scorching kiss. We had to pack up dessert and take it home ... I think it was more tasty the way we had it than the way it was presented at the restaurant.

I sit here now staring at the simple, round, karat-and-a-half diamond set in platinum on my finger. I can't believe it, really. Well, yes actually, I can, but I can't. Does that make sense? Let's see if I can figure this out. I can't believe it because we've only been dating for six months. On the other hand, I can believe it. We've spent nearly every night together since we both got back from Hawaii. We just seem to fit together. Like that Harry Connick Jr. song says, "We go together like a wink and a smile." Garrett is so easy to be around. We can sit and talk for hours about nothing and everything. He's never judgmental or critical when I have a problem or a concern. He just listens. And he makes me laugh, like crack-me-up, crying laughing deep in my belly. Butterflies in my stomach come flying out any time I hear his voice. It's so soft and warm and deep. His eyes are alight with some kind of energy I've never seen before. He has become my everything in such a short amount of time. I'm just crazy, head-over-heels in love with this man, and I can't wait to spend my life getting to know him more and more each day.

A smile spreads across Garrett's face as he remembers that night. He can't believe how radiant Charley sounds from the pages of a book. He's glad to know he gave her such a happy night. He remembers Charley wanting to wait to tell anyone their happy news. She felt they had only been dating such a short amount of time, and they didn't want people to think they were young, reckless kids rushing into anything, especially his parents.

Garrett flips ahead wanting to see what Charley thoughts were when she found out she was pregnant.

I'm pregnant. Not just sort of pregnant. Really pregnant. Like three months pregnant. I had no idea, not one little inkling! I haven't been sick, or had any weird cravings, or anything that would have led me to believe I was pregnant, except for the fact that my pants and my bras were a little snug, but I just chalked that up to eating too much and exercising too little. I went for my annual exam, and my gyno asked, "Do you want to run a pregnancy test?" And that got me thinking, I haven't had a period in maybe three months but didn't really think anything about it — menstrual irregularity is the name of the game when it comes to me. So I told her to go ahead and run it, but I was pretty sure it would come back negative. How stinking WRONG I was! She took me back right away for an ultrasound, and that's when I found out how far along I am. Crazy, Crazy, CRAZY! I saw the heartbeat. The doctor said the baby was developing well. Dr. Wright told me the baby was measuring about 14 weeks. I'm pretty sure the words

"Holy shit" escaped my mouth! She printed out a picture of the baby in utero and gave me all the necessary lectures and paperwork so that I do everything right from here on out. All I can say is that I'm scared shitless right now.

I haven't told Garrett yet. I know we're getting married anyway, but I didn't want it to be like this. We haven't even told anyone about our engagement, and now we have to tell them we're having a baby. Well, shit. This isn't the way I expected things to go. I expected to be a blushing bride and then an expectant mom sometime down the road, but not now. Not yet. What is Garrett going to think?

Garrett turns the page to see what she has to say about the moment she told him. He'll never forget that minute as long as he lives.

Garrett is on cloud nine. He's so happy about our impending "bundle of joy," as he called the baby. I told him to brace himself because I had a really big surprise for him. He let out a whoop of joy and scooped me up in his arms when I showed him the ultrasound picture. He and I enjoyed a quiet afternoon with him exploring my newly ripening belly. I guess the reason my pants are getting a little tight is because of Junior and not too much food. It's a reality. I'm going to be a wife and a mom!

We decided we're getting married in two weeks. We're going to go to the justice of the peace to make it legal. Garrett wants to get married so things are official and settled. Actually, he said he wants to get married so I don't have time to change my mind and run away. Ha ha, like I would walk away from him!

I only ever wanted a small wedding and reception, so this will work perfectly. We will take our witnesses out to dinner afterward, but we will wait to have a party until we're ready, maybe after the baby is born, so we can show off our new sweetheart.

After Garrett dropped me off at home, I called Gayle to tell her the news. To say she was shocked was the understatement of the year, but once she got over her irritation at being kept in the dark about everything (yeah, I didn't tell her about the engagement, in hindsight, I probably should have), I told her to get down to Rebecca's bridal shop. We were going dress shopping! Butterflies hit me hard, and there it came, my first, and hopefully only taste of morning sickness.

I showed up at the shop with my ring on for the first time, and Gayle just about fell over. She hugged me like she's never hugged me before. We found the perfect dresses for both of us. Mine is a simple, white satin dress with long sleeves and a high waist. The neckline plunges about as low as it can, accentuating my growing "assets," while the high waist hides my growing belly. It's perfect. Gayle's is a raspberry-colored dress shaped a little like mine only body skimming and gorgeous. I can't believe this happening so fast.

Garrett remembers Gayle telling him his mom was not so nice to Charley during the days after the wedding and when they told everyone their news about the baby. He needs to see what was said and how Charley explained it. He looks through the next couple of weeks, finally finding what he needs. The words hit him hard.

Well, we told our parents today. Mine were so sad that we didn't share the news ahead of time, but they understood, kind of. They know we are adults and trying to make our own ways in this world. I promised that I would let them host our party for us once we figured out what we wanted to do. They wished us well and congratulations across the miles, promising to come visit soon.

I'm looking forward to that more than anyone can know, especially after how Garrett's mom responded.

We told his parents together. His dad was sweet about it. He clapped Garrett on the back and congratulated him, pulling him into an awkward "guy" hug. He gave me a stiff hug and a kiss on the cheek. Garrett's mom reacted a little differently. She shrieked and yelled at us, asking us how we could do this to her. "What am I supposed to tell my friends?" she wailed at us. Garrett and his dad tried to placate her and tell her everything was going to be fine. She seemed to perk up a little as Garrett showed her a picture of the baby and then changed the subject.

I thought everything was going OK until Garrett and his dad went to look for his old bassinet that was tucked in the attic somewhere. (Garrett's mom was deathly afraid of spiders, so there was no way she was going up there to look, leaving it up to his dad and Garrett to find the old treasure.) When they left, I found out exactly what his mom thinks of me.

We chatted a little while, and I thought everything was going great. She had a smile on her face and was asking questions about me and my upbringing. With that same smile, she said to me, "So, the little gold digger found a way to catch herself a doctor." I was sure I didn't hear her right, so I said, "I beg your pardon?" trying to be polite and ask her to repeat herself. That's when she said, "Honey, don't you beg my pardon ever again. You have no right to be uppity with me." I was stunned. I apologized profusely for sounding like I was being uppity, and I tried to explain that I had always been taught to say, "I beg your pardon" when I couldn't hear what someone had said. My cheeks were on fire, and I needed to escape, so I excused myself and went to find the bathroom. I stayed put until I heard Garrett and his father come back downstairs, and then I pretended I didn't feel well so I could leave. Garrett and I drove separately, so I kissed him good-bye, letting him stay with his parents. I drove myself back to our newly combined apartment.

Garrett came home to check on me and found me crying in the living room. I told him what happened at his parents' house, and he said "Char, my mom wouldn't say that about you! You must have misheard her." He chalked my tears and my "misunderstanding" of his mom up to my pregnancy.

I hope this isn't how things will always be with his mom. I don't want to go through a marriage with a nasty mother-in-law and a son who can't see it, especially because we live so close.

Garrett closes his eyes, and as he remembered that day and Charley crying, a little pang of guilt hits him. He thought he had told her that there was no way his mom could ever say that to her because she's such an amazing woman, and no one would dare say something like that to her. But, as he reads, he remembers he got called into work as they were talking, and he never told her the rest of what was on his mind. She had everything written down, everything his mom said. She wouldn't have included that part if it weren't true.

Garrett can't believe Charley never said anything more to him about what his mom said to her when they got married. Now that he thinks about it, he can believe his mom would have spoken to her that way. He has seen his mother turn mean and vindictive when she's been drinking, but he never imagined she treated Charley in that manner.

He thumbs through the rest of the year. In this year of newness for them, Charley talks about love, the reception, babies, and being a mother of her own child, but not much else about his mom. He wants to sit and read her words so he can hear her voice speaking to him from the pages, but before he can do that, he has to read more about how she started down the path she was traveling to New Orleans.

Gayle had told him where to find most everything. He knows something big happened at his dad's funeral. Gayle had explained to him that Charley was so upset about it at their lunch together. He didn't know exactly what happened in years past, and now he understands. Gayle knew that Garrett needed to hear all of this from Charley's heart.

We just buried Garrett's dad, and at the wake, I buried the desire I once had to be a daughter to his mom. Garrett's dad tried to be kind, but he could never quite overcome his wife's meanness. I know he knew she was an alcoholic, but he did nothing to stop her. He only enabled. I know he had seen and heard some of what she has said to me, but he chose to overlook it, so he could keep her happy. Garrett does the same and has for years. I have tried talking to him about all of this, but he always made excuses or told me she would never say those kinds of things to me. He never believed me. He always chose his mom. I try not to begrudge him a relationship with her. He is her only son, but I'm done trying to be a daughter to her. I'll call when I absolutely have to, but other than that, I'm done.

Today clinched it for me. She accused me of being a whore and getting pregnant on purpose. She told me I slept around and that the twins weren't Garrett's. She said Garrett was trapped into marrying me because I got pregnant and that he would leave me as soon as the kids were grown and gone. Pam told me that I was a gold digger who had slept her way into their family. I was stunned and sickened by her behavior, but I tried hard to chalk it up to grief and despondency from losing her husband. But I can't pretend to have a relationship with her anymore. I am done.

I tried telling Garrett, but he was in no shape for a showdown with his mom. Frankly, I think he would choose her side. He has in the past. He's done it time and time again. There is no reason it would be any different at this point. I can't and won't fight it anymore.

Garrett knows everything she has written is true. There is no reason for her to have made any of this up. She came to him from occasionally about something his mom had said, but she let it drop quickly and had never revisited any of these stories. She never said things like "It's either me or your mom." Ultimatums or threats had never crossed her lips whenever she would talk to him about his mom. She had just stayed away from his parents, and now he understands why. She had taken a lot of verbal abuse from his mom, and she was done having him sweep her story to the side.

His heart constricts as he looks at her frail countenance lying on the bed in front of him. He can't believe she has endured so much and said so little. He can't believe after all of this, she still had the courage to call his mom when he asked her to the other day. He can't believe he has never stood up to his mom for Charley. He has let her down, and he sees that now.

Garrett decides to read a little more of her recent journals. He wants to see more of Charley now. He needs to understand her if they are going to move forward. He feels her anger from two years ago, and it reminds him about how she used to get so mad at him. She used to stand up to him and challenge him. Now that he thinks about it, she stopped fighting with him about two years ago. Charley's taking a stand for making things right between them seems to stop when he failed to stand up for her. He needs to see if he can find it written in her journals.

His eyes begin to burn with unshed tears as he sees lines here and there emphasizing what Charley was trying to get him to hear for years.

How did things get so bad? Ok, maybe bad is the wrong word. Maybe it's just not what I expected. I have a good life, from the outside, anyway. Anyone looking in would think I have the picture-perfect life. My life makes me think of the song He Thinks He'll Keep Her by Mary Chapin Carpenter, where she talks about how she works to keep things looking picture-perfect "spit and polish till it shines," but the girl in the song fell out of love maybe because of the monotony of her daily life and maybe because she didn't get much recognition for who she is as a woman and a lover, only as a mom and a wife. I think I'm becoming the girl in the song.

...

I have to admit, I'm partly to blame for all of this. I used to be the one to pick fights, to try and draw out what was wrong between us and fix the problems. But I'm so tired of feeling like a nag and a shrew, so I stopped. It was always up to me mend things between us. Garrett's happy to bury his head in the sand and let things go.

...

It was exhausting and unrewarding work, so I stopped making an effort in our marriage. I always hoped, though, Garrett would see how empty our marriage was, and that he would want to rebuild it before it was too late.

...

The kids are my world, and I need to focus on them.

...

I am in heaven when they are around. ... It's really only Garrett. He's the void. The empty space in my life. If I let my mind wander back in time, my heart hurts. I see a man and a husband who used to think the world of me and adore me, but that feeling is disappearing day by day. ... But then, I remember the hurt, the pain, and the lack of trying, on Garrett's part, to make things better.

Garrett shakily turns the page to see a poem Charley wrote. How did he not know any of this about Charley? How did he not know she keeps journals like this? How can he not know his wife could write poems? He is stunned as he reads the words to her poem titled "The Questions."

He reads the poem until the end, and a tear silently slips from his eye onto Charley's hand.

We...

Will the "we" continue, Garrett wonders? He doesn't know if they can continue, if Charley will let them.

Maybe she came home early to ask for a divorce. Maybe she realized she had had enough.

CHAPTER ELEVEN

GARRETT IS LOST in his own thoughts when his mom comes bursting into the hospital room with the kids and Gayle in tow.

"How on *earth* could you not tell me about this? I had to learn about this accident from my granddaughter! You don't even have the common courtesy to call and tell me anything. All you care about is *her*," Pam accuses, pointing to Charley lying helpless and broken in the hospital bed, completely dependent on machines to keep her alive.

In that split second, as Garrett looks at his mom with horror, he sees everything Charley has endured for the past seventeen years. His anger and his frustration at never stepping in to protect his wife come washing over him, and he speaks with a ferocity he never could have imagined.

"Do you even *hear* yourself talking, Mother? You sound deluded and irrational. My focus is where it should be in this instance and every instance of my life. My focus is on my wife. Do you see her there? She's in a coma! And *you* come bursting in here demanding why I didn't call you. I didn't call you because I don't know if Charley is going to live or die. I needed to be by her side. She is my 'for better or for worse,' my 'in sickness and in health.' She is my 'until death do us part.' She is my wife. And I can only hope after the way you've treated her for years, and the way I've let you treat her for all of those years, she'll have me back. Now, unless you can add something positive to my world today, I'll have to ask you to leave."

Pam sputters and snorts as she comes close to Garrett. "I've been nothing but nice to that little gold digger. She latched her claws into you as soon as she realized you were a doctor. She was just some lowly, little flight attendant scraping the bottom of the barrel with no money, of course she's gonna hold onto you with all her might. And then she sealed the deal as soon as she got pregnant, and you had to marry her."

"Mother, I said it, and I meant it. Unless you have a positive contribution to make, I'll have to ask you to leave," Garrett demands with a deadly calm. "And you have no idea what you're talking about. Charley is not, and has never been, a gold digger. Charley went to school and got a degree. She became a flight attendant to see the world, to become a bigger-minded person. She wanted to meet and talk to people from all walks of life. She didn't want to end up some petty, old biddy who thinks she has the world by the feet because she belongs to the Junior League. Her family could buy our family five times over, but you would never know it. It took me over a year to figure that out because they never let on. Never. Unlike *you*! You seem to think money is the be-all and end-all. Well, guess what, Mother, it's *not*! And if you had taken ten seconds to come down from your holier-than-thou position to get to know Charley *at all*, you might not be in the sad, sorry place you are right now. But you didn't, and you are."

His mom's eyes grow wide at his words, and she stumbles backward into the wall.

Garrett's voice softens a little as he offers, "Mom, Gayle will drive you home. You need help. It's only eight o'clock in the morning, and you reek of alcohol. If you ever have any desire to be a part of my family again, you will get clean and sober. And just as importantly, if you want to be a part of my family, then you will treat my wife with respect. Now, please leave so I can focus on Charley and getting her well."

As Gayle and his mom are turning to leave the hospital room, Charley's heart monitor lets out a shrill note and goes flat. Garrett's demeanor changes instantly. He transforms from the heartbroken husband to the doctor in charge.

Nurses come flooding into the room as Garrett begins to bark orders. "Gayle, take the kids home, too, *now!*" In the background, he can hear his children starting to cry, and over the low rumble, he hears Andrew's voice calling out, "Mommy, please don't die. Please don't die. Please don't die. I need you."

Garrett tears his gaze away from Charley for one brief minute and sees the tears coursing down the cheeks of their one child who bears an uncanny resemblance to his mother, both in looks and demeanor.

Garrett tries to reassure him, "Andrew, she can hear you. She'll do the best she can, and so will we. But right now, I need you to go, so I can focus on your mom. I love you all, and so does she!"

"My heart is breaking. Charley, honey, please hear me," Gayle pleads. "We need you here with us."

Gayle turns to Pam and says, "Right now, I'm trying very hard to not blame you for her failing heart." On Garrett's instruction, Gayle herds the children and his mom out into the hospital corridors so they can head home.

* * *

Garrett and his team work tirelessly on Charley's heart for twenty minutes. He can't give up on her, not when he is just learning who she really is, after all these years.

His words echo those of his twelve-year-old son, "Charley, please don't die. Please don't die. Please don't die on me. I need you."

Compression after compression and shock after shock go through Charley's tired and battered body until there is finally a spark. Her own heart takes over beating for her, as her vital signs start to stabilize.

Garrett crumples into a chair as soon as he realizes her heart is beating on her own. He is sweating and shaking from the efforts to revive his wife. The tears start sliding down his cheeks, falling silently onto his lap. He can't imagine losing her now.

The mantra running through his head keeps pace with her heartbeat, *Live, Charley. Live, Charley.*

Garrett is beyond exhausted, but he knows he won't leave her side. His place is here, with her. Always.

As he resumes his watch over his wife, Garrett realizes he isn't finished reading. When Gayle came in this morning, her presence reminded him that he hadn't read the tarot card book yet. He wanted to see what Charley believed was so important. As Garrett opens the book, tarot cards and the business card for the marriage encounter fall into his lap. And he knows where his focus should be. He sets the tarot cards to the side. It doesn't matter to him what they say. It only matters to him what Charley has said. He reads what she wrote about the cards in her journals. He knows where they pointed her. They pointed her back to him. What he realized when those cards fell into his lap is how important working on their marriage is, and he knows he has a phone call to make.

He speaks quietly into the phone, explaining his situation to the director of the marriage encounter week and asks for their first available time slot. His heart knows this call is the beginning of Charley coming back to him, in body and spirit. With the arrangements made, he ends the phone call and sits down again at Charley's bedside to keep his vigil.

At some point during the morning, Garrett's head drops wearily onto Charley's hand, and sleep mercifully takes over. He doesn't hear the nurses coming in to check on Charley, nor does he hear Gayle creep in to sit with Charley and keep watch over her while Garrett rests. After several hours of much-needed sleep, Garrett wakes to the sound of the ventilator, and for a brief minute, he forgets where he is.

He looks up to see Gayle sitting in the chair opposite him holding Charley's hand.

Gayle explains, without looking up, "I couldn't stay away. I took the kids to your house. Christina made me promise to call with any information. I dropped your mom off at her own house to sober up and to figure out what she needs to do. I took her inside and wrote down AA's information for her. I hope she calls and gets some help. She doesn't want to lose you."

"No, she doesn't want to lose me, but she doesn't want to accept Charley as my wife, either. That's a deal breaker. Charley is my life, and if I have to choose, I'll choose Charley," Garrett says, his voice thick with unshed tears.

"She's gonna be OK, Garrett. She has too much to live for, to give up now," Gayle replies.

Garrett stifles a sob as tears streak down his cheeks. Gayle comes around the side of the bed and pulls him into her embrace. Until the hug, Garrett hadn't realized how much they need comfort from each other as they watch the one they love so much struggle so hard.

Gayle breaks their embrace. "I know you haven't eaten since before Charley's accident yesterday. I'm going to the cafeteria to get you some lunch. You're running on empty, and Charley is going to need you strong when she wakes up. Do you have any requests?"

Knowing Gayle won't take no for an answer, Garrett replies, "Yes. Can you bring me some soup? I don't care what kind it is—just something warm, please."

Gayle leaves Charley's room as Garrett once again resumes his watch over her. He sits quietly with her for some time just looking at her and realizing how much they both have to lose. His hand has been covering hers as he sits with her. He picks her hand up off the bed and begins to speak softly to her, telling her all of the things he should have been saying all these years.

As his tears spill onto Charley's hand, Garrett's voice gets stronger, "Charley, please don't leave me now. I'm just beginning to relearn who you are. I'm so sorry I let that go for all of these years. You didn't deserve that. You deserved the best of me, but I only gave you what was left over of me. I can't believe I put you last. I can't believe how much I hurt you, and I'm so sorry you didn't hear the loving words from me that you needed to hear. I know you can hear them now, though, and I want you to know you are the most beautiful woman I have ever known. If you could have been in my head when we first met, you would have run the other way thinking I was some lunatic who couldn't believe how lucky I was to find my perfect girl. I couldn't stop thinking about you then, and I wish I would have spent more time telling you how much I think about you now. You are never more than a heartbeat away from my thoughts. God, Charley I wish I had told you how much I love you. Come back to me, so we can make things right between us and grow old together. I want to spend the rest of my days telling you how much I love you."

Garrett is almost certain he feels her hand move in his. It is just a brief flicker, and he knows it could be reflexes, but he has to check.

"Charley, squeeze my hand if you can hear me." He feels it again, just a small contraction, but it is there.

"Charley, come back to me, please," he pleads as a tear slips down his nose on to her hand. He feels her hand tighten around his as he says those words, and he looks up to see the most beautiful set of eyes fixed on him.

Garrett knows he needs to keep her calm. She is intubated, and he doesn't want her panicking or trying to fight the breathing tube in her throat.

"Charley, honey," he begins soothingly, "You were in a very bad accident, and you're in the hospital now. You have a breathing tube in your throat, and we will need to run some tests to see if you will be able to breathe on your own before we can take it out. OK?"

She nods weakly and closes her eyes, falling back to sleep. Garrett is cautiously optimistic as Gayle comes back in the room carrying two cups of soup.

"She moved her hand and briefly opened her eyes while I was talking to her," Garrett excitedly tells Gayle.

"I heard everything you said to her, Garrett. It was beautiful and just what she needed to hear for her to come back. You brought her back," Gayle says wrapping a shaky Garrett in a big bear hug.

"Gayle, I can't lose her now. I know where I screwed up. I know where she screwed up. We both lost sight of what was important in our lives together. I need her to get better so we can get better and back to where we were seventeen years ago," Garrett said. "Stay with her, please. I need to go to the nurses' station and get the neurologist down here so we can try to wake her up again."

EPILOGUE

MAY 30

Garrett and I. We're better. We're not perfect, but I don't want us to strive for perfection. I want us to work towards real and lasting love. The accident was our saving grace. That sounds funny to say, but it's true. My body now bears scars from wounds that have healed now, but the truth is, if it weren't for that semi pulling in front of me, Garrett and I would have festering damage that might never have been repaired. At least we can heal now—together.

I have had a lot of recuperation time and even more time to think. I now realize I was trying so hard to be perfect, to live a perfect life and to expect perfection in every aspect of my marriage that I failed to live outside the confines of a impossible vision of life I created in my head. Good marriages are messy. Great lives are messier. Watching my scars heal and fade taught me that it's healthy to let go of unrealistic versions of perfection I planted in my head.

The marriage encounter was the most grueling week of our lives, and I couldn't be more thankful we had the opportunity to work through it. The time together, reflecting on our marriage and our family, made us both realize that when we work toward balancing each other there is nothing we can't accomplish. We were put into situations where if we didn't work in-sync with one another we weren't able to advance to the next task. The tasks we were asked to do, were tough, but I think the hardest part of the week was having to sit for one minute and look into each other's eyes. I say that was the hardest part because it forced both of us to look into the other's soul. To see, to really see, the love that lives there. A minute might not sound like much, but when you have to look into the eyes of someone you live with, but haven't really felt loved by for years it's a heart stopping experience. The deep, abiding, gut wrenching love pours out in their eyes and back into your own soul. Two hearts become one again.

At the end of all of it, I finally figured out the end to the poem I wrote almost two months ago. I ended it with "We." And I wondered if we, Garrett and I, would continue. Now I know.

We have so many memories and have shared so much time.
We have a long, long hill to climb.
How do we get there?
Where do we go?
I guess these are the questions, we together, will answer, though.
We want this to work. We want to work hard.
We will come out of this a little scarred.
We will work.
We will fight.
We will prevail, and our lives will once again be bright.
I feel in my heart the despair has lifted.
Now we ensure our lives are lived with love gifted.
I fought.
You fought.
We fought together.
We made sure our life together, the storm it would weather.
The storms have been wicked and wild.
But the angels looked down on us and smiled.
We. That is the magic word
Our hearts are melting together as, once again, our love is stirred.

ACKNOWLEDGMENTS

I couldn't have written this book without the help of more people than I can begin to mention. Everyone who stood beside me as I worked and labored over this story holds a special place in my heart. I've had the tremendous fortune of working with an incredible team. Vicki Sly and Amy Oravec, the polishing of this novel couldn't have been accomplished without you. I'd like to offer a special thanks to Dr. Matt. I hope I put your medical knowledge to good use.

My thanks to you all knows no bounds.

Made in the USA
Middletown, DE
31 July 2021